Short Stories by Mike Stone

AF583238

Short Stories

Copyright © 2022 by Michael Stone

All rights reserved

No part of this book may be reproduced or utilized in any form or by any means, electronic or mechanical, including photocopying, recording, or by any information storage and retrieval system without permission in writing.

Inquiries should be addressed to:
Mike Stone
email: mike.stone.email@gmail.com

Contents

Foreword

What inanimate objects have souls?

Why, books, of course.

Scientists talk about the possibility one day of uploading our minds to digital repositories or AI algorithms, but writers and poets have been uploading their souls to books for hundreds of years already.

You'll see those souls peeping out of each of the stories in this book.

Some of the stories are fictional, like "Investigations of a Kafkaesque Nature" about the philosophical ruminations of a dog, "An Idea for a Short Story" about a man who has suffered a stroke and comes out of it after his granddaughter reads him his poems, and "A Walk in the Desert" about a man who gets lost in the desert, has a friendly argument with God, and is rescued by those he thought were coming to kill him.

Some of the stories are biographical, like "Grandma", about the strong, loving woman, with whom our parents deposited us when they went on their summer vacations, "Getting into Trouble", about the time my friend and I took a bus to an amusement park in another town and had to walk back home because we'd spent too much money on rides and hotdogs, and "Dancing with Anna" about the time my wife asked me if I'd like to invite the beautiful salon dancer, Anna A., to our home to teach me how to dance, and I said yes, which my wife did not expect.

Some of the stories are semi-biographical, like

"Transmigration of a Soul", about how a little while after our boxer, Daisy, died, a fly flew into my work room and remained close to me, without flitting away as flies usually do, "The Treasure Chest", about a small box shaped like a pirate's treasure chest, to which our grandkids would run to, pull out coins I had collected during my travels to foreign countries, and ask me to tell them what I did in those countries, and "Beshert" about the unexpected destiny I followed from an Ohio childhood, to a blind-date with an Israeli girl, whom I ended up marrying, and emigrating to Israel.

Then there are the "One-Eighth Cherokee" stories, which I wrote after finding out my grandma's mother might have been a Cherokee. Although I haven't requested a DNA check to discover whether I really have Cherokee blood in me, the idea inspired me to write those sixteen stories, all of them fruit of my wild imagination.

Since I've lived over half of my life in Israel, I tend to think of the Mediterranean Sea as my personal puddle; Hence, the fifteen stories of "All along the Mediterranean", which take place in Israel (of course), Greece, Ethiopia (when we were all still Africans). Some of those stories spring from myths and others spring from my own breast.

Happy reading!

Grandma

Days of summer are golden, and nights are silken, when you're a kid. They float through your childhood like leaves down a dark stream, and endless hours flit by like butterflies. I remember the crunch of gravel under our tires, as Dad drove us up the driveway to leave us with Grandma for the summer. Those were the best of days along with the delicious anticipation beforehand.

Grandma would come out the back porch door to greet us, the skin sagging from her ample arms, and dishtowel in hand. Almost before our car had stopped, we'd spill out and run to her, hugging her with our faces pressed hard to her apron, from not seeing her since the summer before.
We'd be walking, the three of us, through the backdoor into the smells of fried chicken, applesauce, and boiled corn in the kitchen, oblivious to the crunch of gravel outside, as Dad backed our car down the driveway to go on their vacation. We got the better deal, I always thought.

Grandma was a feisty old lady, and everybody said so. She was strong as all get out, and there were two things she wouldn't stand for: sass and nonsense.

She had a slightly dipping limp, like Hephaestus, the Greek blacksmith god (I think she stored her strength there, inside her limp).

Grandpa number three (Grandma legally buried all the rest) had an old DeSoto with a knob on the steering wheel that you could turn real easy backing out their driveway. He'd let me sit on his lap and steer the car while his feet pressed the gas or brakes, back and forth on the crunchy driveway almost to the neighbor's trailer.

Come to think of it, Grandma only allowed herself one little nonsense in all her life: when she'd watch tee-vee with all of us, sitting around her on the floor, she'd be watching Liberace playing his piano, and he'd always turn around and wink at Grandma, or so she thought.

I remember a promise I made her: when I'd grow up, I'd buy a big white limousine, and I'd come by and pick her up and drive her 'round town.

I never kept that promise, and the sorrow of it will follow me like a sad little dog to my grave, wherever that may be.

Getting into Trouble

Sometimes you have to get into trouble, just to make it through your childhood in one piece.

I had a friend, growing up, not so much a friend, maybe, but one of the kids who didn't beat me up, though he could have. I remember wondering why, at the time, that was, and thought it might be because we both had the same first name.

He had a pack of cigarettes rolled up in the sleeve of his tee-shirt, showing his thin (but taut) muscles. This was back when we lived in San Diego.

My friend and I decided to go to Mission Bay Park, which was an hour or so bus ride from school. My parents said I had to be back by supper, but I kept that to myself, since my friend didn't have any such limitations.

We counted our money and figured how much we had for bus fare, back and forth, and rides and food.

I don't remember what rides we rode, but I think we had a good time and enough coke and hotdogs.

One thing led to another and, when it came time to head back home, the coins just wouldn't add up to what we needed for bus fare home.

We walked and walked through fields and towns, and suburbs and backyards I'd never been in before.

I'd reckon it was around bedtime, if I'd ever been allowed to stay up so late, when I finally got home.

I never saw my friend again. He wasn't the kind of guy you could invite over for a game of chess or ping-pong.

I often wonder what happened to him, and think he'd be surprised to know some guy in some distant country had written a story about him.

Pilgrim's Progress

(*a personal allegory inspired by Sabine Huynh*)

It was time for Daisy's evening walk. We left the apartment, descended in the elevator, and soon we were outside walking our usual walk.

There wasn't much to report along the way, except for the Wolf Moon lunar eclipse and a young girl wearing a backpack walking past us. Daisy did her stuff and we returned home, ascending the elevator, and I put the key in the door.

The Land of Certain Memories

I opened the door to our apartment, but it wasn't our apartment.

A runway spread backwards from the open cargo doors and lowered ramp of a C-130 wavering in the heated air behind the whirling propellers. I walked down the ramp, got into a jeep, and was driven around to the front of the airport where I ascended one of the buses.

After a while I descended from the bus and walked to a wide boulevard lined with arching Ficus trees.

I entered a building, walked up the stairs, and knocked on the door, which was opened by a young woman with long black hair as thick as night.

I entered

The Land of Uncertain Memories

And got off the train as it pulled into the Hauptbahnhoff

Glanced at the wall clock - a little after three in the morning. The night air was chill when I began walking down Ernst Ludwig Strasse toward the barracks.

By the time I passed the guard at the barricade the sun was rising further down the road. I quickly changed into my greens and rushed out to the courtyard to stand reveille formation with everyone else

The Land of Inaccessible Memories

But there was nobody else in the courtyard.

My little sister stood next to me, looking up at me and holding my hand. My father and stepmother stood in front of us.

We were inside a small brick apartment. They told us our mother had just died, she never really loved us though, and would we like to go out and play?

I opened the screen door and went outside.

A young woman without arms stood on the other side of the street. I ran to hug her to feel her warmth but

The Land of the Forgotten Memories

I was standing in the backyard, sloping down to a leafy ravine.

I was looking at a small log cabin my father had built for me, halfway up the hill beyond the ravine.

I walked down the hill and up the next hill to the cabin, ducked my head, and went inside.

My mother was sitting in a rocking chair, holding an infant against her breast and singing to the smiling child.

I recognized what she is singing, but I couldn't hear her voice.

I asked her to let me hear her voice once more, just once, please, just one time more, but they could only see and hear each other.

The Land of Imagined Memories

She's five years old, riding on my shoulders, squealing joyfully about winning some race as we pass my wife on the way to our parked car.

No, Saba, I can buckle my own seatbelt!

She corrects my Hebrew mistakes, twinkling her eyes each time.

We pull into her parents' driveway, and she's unbuckled and out of the car before I can turn around.

Let me hear her voice once more, just once, please, just one time more.

Investigations of a Kafkaesque Nature

I'm running through a lush field of yellow grass blades after a black cat under a blue sky. The cat jinks this way and that but I'm gaining on him. I've never run so fast in my life. It's like I'm flying over the grasses and through the bushes. It's like I'm synchronized with all motion and I'm lying still inside the motion while the universe is doing the running and the cat and I are one with it, but I am getting closer. From far away I feel something warm on my twitching muscles and jerk to attention, but it is the calming hand of my human, soothing me but insisting that I awaken. The cat, the grasses, and the universe dissipate. They are replaced by another reality. My human touches a square on the wall of our cave and the eyelids open slowly, letting in the morning light. He brings the chain linked collar and long strap to put around my neck, but I lay my head down, feigning sleep. It's a game I play before we go out for my walk which, feeling my kidneys full once more, it's probably time for. I rise to my feet, and we walk to the mouth of our cave. My human sticks something into a small hole in the wall which opens sideways. We leave the cave and walk down the steppingstones to another eyelid which my human opens. We walk down more steppingstones to a path in which big blue, yellow, and grey metal insects roll noisily past on dark rubber feet. Of course, I would prefer to run freely instead of being constrained by the chain and strap, but I don't know whether my human needs the strap for me to pull him along or he's afraid I'll run into the path of those big rolling insects. I don't want him to worry about me, since worry smells like fear which is a sign of weakness, and I don't want him to be weak. Sometimes my human doesn't seem to know what's good for him. When I smell a stranger who is menacing or afraid, I know it is up to no good and I'd better lunge at him before he attack us, but my human yanks on my chain and strap when I'm already in midair. It can be so embarrassing and frustrating. We walk by the stranger, and I feel so cowed, but nothing bad happens this time. It might have. Always attack first is my policy. It's safer. The world is a dangerous place and if you want to survive in it, you have to keep your wits about you. A walk in the park is not necessarily a walk in the park, if you know what I mean. My human is too trusting and one of these days I won't be able to protect him.

We start our walk, but I get easily sidetracked in the here and now. There are so many stories to listen to and you can never know in advance which ones will be only just very interesting and which ones will be whoa I can't move another inch before I hear the rest of it, like this scrawny grey-yellow bush in the garden we almost passed by. A human who had just birthed two human pups had passed by and left their scents worth on the leaves. One of the pups didn't take his mother's milk so well. It might be related to the acrid smell of his urine. This takes time and I need more information, but my human is trying to pull me away already. I try to convey to him that this is important, but he doesn't seem to understand. Honestly, sometimes I don't know what they're thinking inside those inflated brains. I squirt a bit of urine near the spot to mark how far I'd gotten in this saga, so I don't have to start from the beginning next time around. The human and I always walk the same path, two or three times a day, but sometimes it's not the same path because the smells are new. It's the same but not the same. Go try to explain that to a creature who walks upright. It's as though they don't want to smell the world around them. Keep your nose to the ground I always say. We continue our walk and I sniff what I can. Somebody has to do the smelling around here.

Suddenly my bowels feel full, and I release them. My human scoops it up in a bag and tosses it into a round container. Honestly, I don't know why I bother to do it. It's such a waste of time.

As we continue our walk, we enter a cloud of digital emanations leaking out of the eye of a cave near us. Although the noise is annoying to me, it doesn't seem to bother my human who is tapping with his thumbs on some small slab of plastic. The cloud contains an article on quantum physics and human irrationality. It states that although modern humans have attempted to base their rationality on the logical and mathematical models of Aristotle, that a thing either is or is not something, but the article goes on to say that our world is really a large number of states that can be and not be at the same time, at least until you measure them. Once you measure them and depending on how you measure them, they become one state or another. Quantum physics is a bit beyond me but it seems to me that logic and mathematics only derive their value from the premise that they somehow reflect how our physical world really works. If not, then what are they good for? I don't believe in total chaos. The world kind of makes sense to me. Neither do I believe in a big dog in the sky who created this world and everything that happens depends on Its will or whimsy.

We passed through the cloud and continued our walk. My bladder was still half full, but I had to save some of my urine for come what may. My human avoids other dogs, cats, and people when we walk together. I worry about his social life. Finally, our path takes us to the mouth of our cave. He puts his stick into the mouth so it will open. Then he pushes a square next to another mouth. I sit patiently beside him waiting for the mouth to open. When it finally does, we enter a small cave that's not our cave yet. My human presses another square and the cave begins to jiggle and vibrate. Soon it stops and the mouth opens. I walk to the mouth of our cave and wait for my human to put another stick in the mouth of our cave. The mouth opens and we are home.

That's all I wanted to be.

Transmigration of a Soul

I'm not saying that I believe in the transmigration of souls, but a few months after Daisy died, a fly must have come in through an open window, because I noticed it on the wall by my desk.

Normally I shoo flies away whenever I see them, but this time, something softened in my heart, and I couldn't bring myself to do it.

I returned to my writing and, the next time I looked up, the fly was still on the wall. Slowly I placed my hand on the wall next to the fly, but it did not flit away as flies often do. I lowered my hand.

Later that night I closed the window, turned off the light, and went to bed.

In the morning, the fly was still there, so I opened the window and returned to my writing, but the fly stayed on the wall beside me.

This continued for several days, until one morning when I came into the room, I found the fly on its back unmoving. Again, something softened in my heart.

I gently lifted the fly in my hand, took it outside, and laid it among the blades of cool grass.

I don't know why I thought of this just now, but maybe death comes back, once in a while, to softly remind us of love's loss and transmigration.

Elvira

He flipped through the record albums, looking for that one, the one he listened to at times like these, until he found it: Mozart's Piano Concerto, Number twenty-one, in C Major.

He laid the record gently on the turntable, aligning the record hole and turntable spindle. He raised the tonearm and lowered the needle, carefully over the second band, the Second Movement, the Andante, "Elvira Madigan". He preferred the minor keys.

He sat down beside the phonograph, eyes closed, and conducted the concerto dreamily with a raised index finger, slower and slower, until his finger was out of sync with the distant music from the speakers.

He remembered the last scene, a grainy photograph, a shot, and then another shot.

He remembered the young girl with whom he had seen the movie, nothing so dramatic as the two shots, but she was dead too, cancer, so unceremoniously.

Enough of gestures and ceremonies, he thought.

The needle skidded against the inner spiral of the record label, over and over, and over and over.

An Idea for a Short Story

Sounds.
Voices.
Tingling.

"I saw a twitch ..."

"... His eyelids are fluttering ..."

"How are we doing today Mr. Stavros? You gave us quite a scare, didn't he Mrs. Stavros?"

The young woman addressing him was dressed in a pale blue pajama holding a clipboard with pen poised to note something indicative. Off to the left side of his visual space was an older woman who seemed to stare intently at him. The younger woman was more attractive than the older woman, so his eyes shifted back in her direction. On the right side of his visual field were two young men. One was sitting and the other was standing.

Suddenly the door burst open, and another young man entered the room. "I got here as quickly as I could," he said looking at me for some unfathomable reason. He came close to me and put his lips to my cheek, funny I couldn't feel it, and squeezed my arms with his hands.

The older woman was leaning forward in her chair and holding my hand. I saw this but I couldn't feel it either. "It's good you came but prepare yourself," one of the young men said, vacating his chair for the new man who had just entered. "He doesn't seem to recognize any of us and he can't feel anything on his left side."

"Hush," the older woman said to one of the men. "He'll hear you and ..." She burst into tears. "I can't anymore," she sobbed and got up from her chair to leave the room.

I wasn't sure whom they were talking about, and I had no idea who they were.

"Good morning Mr. Stavros," an attractive young woman in pale blue pajamas said in his direction. "How are we this morning? Time for us to turn you over ... Just you let us do the work."

There was another sturdier woman in dark blue pajamas on the other side of his vision he hadn't noticed before. They lifted him onto his side. The older woman from the day before was sitting on the chair next to his bed. He heard voices behind him.

He wondered who these people were. Why did that attractive young woman call him Mr. Stavros? Why was the older woman calling him Joe? Why were the young men calling him Dad?

"Good morning Mr. Stavros," the young woman from the other day said to him. "How are we doing today? You have a special visitor today."

A young girl entered the room cautiously. She couldn't have been more than twelve or thirteen. She looked at me, then at one of the young men, and finally back at me. She came over to the bed, said "Hi Grampa", kissed my cheek which I still couldn't feel, and lay her head on my chest. Her long hair spread over my chest and smelled like ... like ... what was it? Who was she?

The young girl pulled up a chair near the bed and took out a thin book from a backpack. She opened the book and started reading out loud, "An Idea for a Short Story, August 22, 2014, Sounds. Voices. Tingling."

"What are you doing Cory?" one of the young men asked her.

She looked up from the book and answered, "I got the idea from Grampa. He wrote this story just before he had this ..."

"Stroke?" the young man suggested. "Let me see the story." He had been too busy to read his father's rather prolific writings lately, but he had been meaning to get around to it sometime or other. He read the story over quickly. Then he read it again, this time more slowly. "You had the right idea," he said after rereading it, "but in the story he suggested we read him his poetry books. He said that was where he stored his images and memories. It's worth a try."

"Good morning Mr. Stavros," a young woman said to him from behind her clipboard. "How are we doing today? Your special visitor has come back to see you."

The young girl from the other day came into the room, walked over to the bed, kissed his cheek, and sat down in the chair. She pulled another thin book, this one black, from her backpack and opened it up to the first page. She began to read to him.

Song of Symbols

University years (Michigan State University): 1965-1969

It is a song of symbols,
Clocks and stars;
A string tied to a rock,
At the other end, a kite.

One small blue wildflower
On this slow grassy hill,
A little like Noellen, I think.

The young girl looked up at him from the book and then over at the young man. "His face hasn't changed."

The young man said to her gently, "keep trying". The other two young men said "yeh, keep trying." The older woman studied his face intently, her eyes brimming with tears.

The young girl looked down at the book and turned a page. She began to read aloud.

What They Mean

Northwestern University, Evanston Illinois, Autumn 1969

Whenever you walk among the softened copper leaves
On a wispy smoked autumn morning,
See the dim face of a sun eight minutes old,
Feel the warmcool paradox in your body's secret hiding places,
Hear the gentle shivering at the tops of tall trees,
And possibly wonder what they all mean --
Why, they mean I love you.

She looked up at him. They all looked at him. She looked back down at the book and turned the page.

The Midnight Falls

Indianapolis Indiana 1972

The midnight falls in silent raindrops
From my greylit window forever.
Cars pass through the street in distant sound
And walkers push their hearts against the cold.
Inside my room I hear the sounds of my wife
As she sits upon my bed adjusting her stockings.

I watch her in the mirror above the bureau.
Outside are puddles and reflections.
I am sprawled upon the bed
And run my fingers gently over her white slip
Remembering I am only a child,
A child dreaming of his own family,
Dreaming in a greylit window.

His pupils dilated and his hand twitched inside the hand of the older woman.

"Did you see that?" one of the young men asked.

The older woman said "I felt something, his hand ..."

The young girl flipped through some pages until she found what she was looking for. She began to read again.

Phantom Limbs

Duluth Georgia, March 28, 2014

He felt ambiguated
Yes, he thought, that might be the word.
His unbounded happiness had saddened him.
After all, it was bounded
By the foreshortening of his life
From his perspective.
His wide unwieldy wings ached
To enfold his young granddaughter
Whose hair smelt of fresh wheat on a summer hillock.
He wanted to take her in his arms,
His heavy wings thrumping the air
Until slowly rising above the treetops
One with the cobalt sky
They'd soar and swoop

Over quilted fields and shadowed valleys,
Then back for tea and hoops
And lessons.
Back at home
Sometime during the night,
Or was it when he woke?
His wings were gone
But the ache remained
Like phantom limbs.

A tear welled up in his eyes and spilled down his cheeks. He squeezed his wife's hand and turned his eyes toward his lovely granddaughter. His sons surrounded their mother, comforting her sobs.

How Will I Know When I'm an Adult?

"How will I know when I'm an adult Saba?" the boy asked his grandfather. The grandfather looked into his inviting blue eyes, pools of clear water, careful not to fall into them.

"Do you want the answer all adults give to their children, or do you want my answer?" the saba asked his eleven-year-old grandson, whose named happened to be Daniel, but this saba did not believe in chance. Daniel meant "God has judged me" in Hebrew, but every Hebrew name means something. One can't escape from meaning in this country.

"I want your answer Saba," Daniel said. His eyes flashed and he grinned.

The saba wondered how he did that. He didn't answer right away. Rather he looked off into the distance, probably for the right answer to his grandson's question. "You want to be an adult, yes?" the saba asked. That's the way people in this country asked questions: they made a factual statement, ending it with yes? Or no?

Daniel said, "Sure, everyone my age wants to be an adult already."

"Well," Saba said, "if you want to be an adult, then you're not one yet. As soon as you want to be a kid again, that's when you'll know you're an adult."

Somewhat disappointed by Saba's answer, not because it didn't ring true, but because it did, Daniel asked, "Okay, give me another sign so that I can know."

"Well," Saba said again, "do you love your children?"

"But Saba," Daniel protested, "I don't have any children! You know that, don't you? I'm just eleven years old. Besides, you have to be married, like Mom and Dad, to have children."

Saba was waiting in ambush for Daniel to say that. "When you're an adult, you love your children more than you love yourself."

"Oh," Daniel said despondently, "I see. Give me one last sign, Saba, please."

"Well," Saba said yet another time, drawing this out as much as possible, "do you like coffee or whiskey?"

"I hate those things, Saba!" Daniel said. "I don't know how adults can like those drinks. Besides, what do they have to do with being an adult?"

"When you drink coffee or whiskey, not because you're thinking about drinking coffee or whiskey, but because it makes you think about something else so far away, it's over the horizon, then that'll be a sign," the saba paused to take a sip of scalding tea and lemon, crinkling his eyes toward the dipping sun, "unless, of course, you don't drink coffee or whiskey, and then it won't matter."

Daniel pondered his saba's words for a long time. "Saba," he said, "you knew I wouldn't understand anything you would answer, right?"

Saba answered, "Well, yes, I suppose I did."

"So why did you answer me?" Daniel asked.

"Because you asked," Saba winked.

The Jungle

The jungle slept fitfully at night. It dreamt dreams of hunger and satiation, crawling around on its belly, running swiftly on its bare feet, and flying through the moist warm air blindly with only its sensitive hearing to guide it. Under the gibbous moon the jungle hooted and cawed in its sleep. Ever so little by little the dome of sky would lighten over the sleeping jungle until the sun would burn a hole through the dreams and the swarms of myriad small buzzings. Then the jungle would wake up into a new day full of great new expectations but also knowing that the day was much the same as other days that came and went. The jungle had pretty much everything it wanted. It was never lonely and there was no other place it wanted to go.

But one day there was something new in the jungle. It was suddenly curious whether there might be other jungles or things it could not even imagine in its dreams. The jungle decided it would go outside of itself to see what it could see. A long tubule extended from the jungle over many walking bare feet. The tubule wended and meandered its way through the forests, over creeks and grassy savannahs, and under the domes of day and night until it came to a small wooden cave grazing the nectar of buttercups in the sunlight. The tubule looked through a square frame of open space along the side of the wooden cave. It didn't see anything particularly dangerous, so it gently pushed open the door and entered the cave. There were many things inside it did not recognize so it climbed up the stairs and pushed open another door. It saw another square frame of open space and approached.

The tubule had intended to look through the frame to see what was on the other side but instead it saw a funny creature in the middle of the frame looking back at it. The creature seemed to be detached from the jungle, a singularly lonely being, defined as much by what he was as what he was not.

The creature said to himself 'I will call myself a man from now on, something separate from the jungle which I now only vaguely remember, which I will one day tame and then beat back. I will call this new thing in which I live civilization and civilization will beat back the jungle until it gasps its last breath.'

The jungle felt a wince of pain from its lost tubule and hunched itself smaller, shaking until the night dome of the moon and stars soothed it with dreams of hoots and caws.

A Walk in the Desert

Tuvi Ornat put the old concert ticket he'd been using as a bookmark between the two pages he had been reading and laid the dog-eared paperback gently on the table beside his chair. He stood up and stretched his arms.

"I'm going for a walk," Tuvi called upstairs but there was no response. He scribbled a short note and slid a small corner of it beneath her tea mug on the kitchen table where she'd be sure to see it when she returned. He buckled a fanny pack around his waist and placed his keys and wallet in the zippered pockets. He put a notebook, pen, and the book he was reading in an old backpack one of his sons had left at home. Tuvi locked the door and walked outside.

It was a pleasant enough day, not too warm and not too cool. The few clouds in the pale blue sky were wispy like feathers. Tuvi walked past the manicured parkways and gardens. Palm tree fronds wavered slightly in the light breeze. He reached the main road and walked over to the shaded bus stop. Tuvi pulled his book out of his backpack while he waited for the bus. He only managed to read a paragraph before the bus arrived and opened its accordion doors. He climbed the three steps, paid the driver, saw a seat in the middle of the bus where nobody was sitting, and sat down looking around at the other passengers. A pretty young mother was sitting with her little boy who wore rather thick glasses. She looked like she might be religious because of the sleeves, but you couldn't be certain with women. Tuvi smiled at the little boy, reached across, and handed him a wrapped candy. "What do you say?" the young mother asked her son prettily. The little boy asked, "Can I have another one?" Tuvi retrieved another candy from his pocket and handed it over to the little boy's extended hand. The mother looked embarrassed and then out the window. Tuvi also looked out his window and watched the stores and pedestrians flow by.

The bus arrived at the central station and Tuvi followed the mother and little boy out the rear doors of the bus. He stopped at the large sign and looked for his destination. He saw the platform number and walked towards his bus. There was a group of young soldiers milling around the open baggage doors of the bus. They had their rifles slung over their shoulders this way and that. They looked so nice, the boys and girls, but they looked so young. Tuvi knew that meant he was getting older. He was glad they were travelling with him on this bus, but it probably meant he'd have to stand most of the way until they reached the large army base just before he wanted to get off, unless one of them would be kind enough to give him his or her seat. The trouble was that Tuvi didn't look his age. People always thought he was much younger although he didn't always feel younger inside. Tuvi grabbed the overhead bar when the driver closed the pneumatic doors with a wheeze, and the bus lurched backwards as it pulled away from the platform.

Soon the bus left the town, turning onto the highway going south. The orchards and fields on either side of the speeding bus were a palette of mostly greens and browns. Tuvi wondered how the farmers would get by this year, the seventh year in which the land was to be left fallow and not to be worked. The principle made sense to Tuvi, but the application of it in this country did not. He thought leaving a seventh of your farmland fallow and then rotating your crops made more sense than farming all your land six years and leaving it fallow in the seventh. Suppose there were a drought or too much rain in the sixth year?

The bus stopped at a crossroads near a small town. Two soldiers got off the bus and collected their duffle bags from under the bus. There was an empty seat next to a pretty girl soldier sleeping with her head against the window. Tuvi sat down gratefully. The bus picked up speed once more. He looked out the window and noticed that the green fields had been replaced by dry brush and long stretches of sand. Tuvi took out his book and opened it across his knees. The girl soldier shifted her head against the seat back, an inch from his shoulder. A few strands of her thick blonde hair brushed his arm, or so he thought. Tuvi didn't want to look for fear of waking her. He relaxed back in his seat and closed his eyes.

Tuvi woke suddenly. The bus had stopped, and the soldiers were milling toward the rear door of the bus. "Hey Kira, we've arrived," someone said. "Stop molesting the old guy!" The blonde-haired soldier sitting next to him sat up straight, turned in Tuvi's direction, and said, "Excuse me." Tuvi stood up next to his chair so that she could exit with her friends. He watched them collect their duffle bags and start walking toward the gates of the large base. A veiled woman wearing a burka over jeans and sneakers, three children, and several bearded men wearing large knit skull caps entered the bus and sat down in the front seats. Tuvi eyed them suspiciously. He couldn't be certain whether they were one of us or one of them because he wasn't born here. The bus started to move.

The rocky sandy landscape undulated as it flashed past the window like images in an old-fashioned zoetrope. Dilapidated pickup trucks and young dark-skinned boys sitting on carts flicking switches on the backsides of lazy mules exited Tuvi's field of vision as quickly as they had entered it. A patchwork of tents and corrugated siding dotted the hills in the middle distance away from the road. He noticed television antennae poking out of the center of most tents. The bus slowed down and stopped at a traffic light. A young boy was selling hot pretzels at the intersection while a couple elders played shesh-besh in the shade of the bus stop. The light changed and the bus started up.

Soon the bus began its slow deliberate descent down a series of narrow hairpin curves with sheer mountainous walls on one side of the bus and the ground dropping away steeply on the other side. The veiled woman held her children tight against her while the bearded men murmured conspiratorially in a tongue Tuvi did not recognize.

Finally, the bus came out onto a wide straight stretch of road toward the great salt sea that could be seen in the distance. The bus slowed and stopped at the side of the road, unremarkable except for a rusted pole and sign indicating the way to the Qumran caves. Tuvi stood up and walked unsteadily down the steps of the bus into the furnace of desert air. He walked toward a stand of trees wavering in and out of the heated air like a mirage. When he reached the shade of trees, he stopped to stretch his legs and turned back toward the road. The bus had already disappeared from sight and the road was also wavering in and out of vision like something not quite substantial. He noticed that one of the bearded men had gotten off the bus with him and had paused halfway between the road and where Tuvi stood to light up a cigarette between cupped hands.

Tuvi turned around away from the road and followed the path beyond the stand, down the hill, and around the bend with his eyes. There wasn't much difference between the path and not the path. He'd come this far, and he'd go a bit further. Tuvi wished he'd taken along a few bottles of mineral water. Maybe there'd be some further on. He started walking down the path on the other side of the stand of trees, down the hill, and around the bend. He noticed the rocky hillsides had changed their hues to white and ochre from the abundance of lime and sulfur in this area. Tuvi also noticed that the bearded man had also started down the same path about fifty yards behind him.

Tuvi continued walking. The path led through a narrow gap between two tall cliffs. Yea though I walk through the valley of the shadow, he thought to himself. Good place for an ambush. The path climbed up some flat stones that formed a natural stairway. Tuvi followed the path to the top of a low promontory and looked back the way he came. The bearded man was sitting on a grey-white boulder about the same distance from Tuvi as before, smoking, flicking ashes on the ground, and looking off into the distance. He stubbed his cigarette into the path and continued towards Tuvi.

Tuvi started walking up the hill. Foot paths crisscrossed each other every so often. Beside most path crossings Tuvi encountered a pile of stones, sometimes placed one on top of the other and sometimes put in a sort of pyramid, but there were other patterns as well. He had heard that the Bedouins construct and use them as markers to help them find their way across the mountains and valleys of the desert, say, to a village or well. Tuvi thought it was interesting how the Bedouin used the rocks as a language that allowed them to understand what the desert was telling them. Everyone knew they were expert scouts and trackers in the desert because they knew the place of every rock and when a rock was out of place. The rock piles were no use to Tuvi, however, and so he continued up the path he chose to follow as best he could.

Tuvi climbed the hill. When he reached the top he turned around to look for the bearded man, but he was nowhere to be found. Tuvi turned back around and looked at the wide expanse of valley at the bottom of the hill. Off a ways craggy mountains grew on either side of the valley. The mountain sides were spotted with caves. He selected one of the caves that seemed accessible without a rope and climbing gear and walked down the sandy hill toward it.

When he reached the ledge in front of the cave, Tuvi ducked his head and looked into the inviting shadow. He walked in, a few paces, hunched over to avoid bumping his head against the rocky ceiling. He didn't see any bats or scorpions around, so he sat down on one of the flat rocks jutting from the wall. He looked out from the cave toward the low western mountain tops. The sun was just about to touch the top crags.

Suddenly Tuvi felt very tired. He bent down to smooth away some of the rocks and twigs on the ground in front of him, lay his backpack down like a pillow, and stretched himself out carefully on the ground. Just a little snooze never hurt anyone, was the last thing he thought about before drifting off to sleep.

"You really should have brought along a few bottles of water," a voice interrupted Tuvi's sleep.

Tuvi woke up with a start. It was pitch dark all around him. He felt around with his hand for the flat rock he'd been sitting on before he'd decided to take a snooze. With his hand still on the flat rock, he sat up painfully, his back stiff with aching. He stood up carefully, remembering the low cave ceiling, swiveled around, and managed to sit down. "What did you say?" he asked.

"You really should have brought along a few bottles of water."

"Tell me about it," Tuvi said sarcastically.

"I just did."

"Where are you," Tuvi asked, "I can't see in this dark."

"I'm everywhere".

"Are you threatening me?" Tuvi asked testily.

"No, not really, though I could have struck you dead, killed you, whatever, at several points along the way, if I'd wanted to. The bus could've blown a tire going around one of those hairpin curves or that bearded gentleman could have come up behind you and slit your throat. Maybe he still will."

"Who are you?" Tuvi asked, not knowing where to face.

"Who do you think?"

"I think you're a nut who thinks he's God," Tuvi answered, "or a crook running a scam. That's what I think."

"Are you an atheist?"

"You should know," Tuvi answered.

"Yeh, I thought so."

"Not really," Tuvi softened his voice. "I'm more of an agnostic. I don't have any evidence one way or the other."

"I know what an agnostic is."

"Sorry," Tuvi said, "I didn't mean to insult you."

"You're pretty polite. Does that mean you're afraid of me?"

"No," Tuvi responded, "that's just the way I was raised to be."

"Ah, so there's not much of a chance that you'll be worshipping me anytime soon?"

"Sorry, no," Tuvi answered.

"Why?"

"Because there's not much about you that's worthy of worship," Tuvi said, and then he asked, "When's the last time you were in a synagogue, church, or mosque?"

"Never been in one."

"So, you have no idea what people are saying in your name?" Tuvi asked.

"Not really. No. What are they saying about me?"

Tuvi collected his thoughts before answering, "They say that you're a jealous god, that you demand our obedience, that you're always testing our faith in you, that we were born in sin, that we should kill those who don't believe in you, that you made us masters of all that you created, that we shouldn't eat pork, that we shouldn't mix meat with milk, that we shouldn't wear jeans, ..."

"I said all those things? Sounds pretty self-serving to me."

"That's what I've been thinking," Tuvi said. "Why would a god of the whole universe micromanage like that, especially in such a juvenile manner?"

"Now that we have that settled, you seem like you have a pretty good head on your shoulders. What are we going to do about getting you rescued?"

"How about you?" Tuvi asked.

"Don't look at me. I can't create a boulder so heavy that even I can't lift it and, just between you and me, I can't even lift a tiny pebble off the ground. Whisking you back to the bus stop and making the bus come to collect you is a bit beyond my abilities."

"Maybe some soldiers will come to rescue me," Tuvi offered half-heartedly.

"Did you let anyone know where you're going or when you should be back?"

Tuvi told him about the note he'd left for his wife on the kitchen table.

"What did it say?"

Tuvi answered, "That I was going for a walk."

"That's it?"

"Pretty much so," Tuvi said.

"Nothing about where or when you'd be back?"

"No," Tuvi said softly. "It doesn't matter."

"Why's that?"

Tuvi said, "She's been gone a year now."

"I see."

Tuvi didn't say anything for a while. It was starting to get chilly in his cave. He was starting to get a bit of a headache too. It was kind of a shame. He hadn't intended for things to end this way. He wondered what way that would be.

Tuvi heard them before he saw them, the whistles and ululations. Then he saw what looked at first like fireflies in the distance. The whistling and shouts were getting stronger, louder. The fireflies turned into torches lighting up faces and arms. "Oh," he said to himself, "so that was how it was going to be."

Suddenly two men stood at the entrance to the cave. They were holding torches. It was hard to tell from the flickering light, the way it danced on their faces, but it seemed to Tuvi that one of them was the bearded man he'd seen following him from the bus. The bearded man shouted something indecipherable to someone else on his right.

The cave filled with the light of the torches as two men entered hunched over carrying a blanket and plastic bottles of mineral water.

Something Happened

Charlie Jones attended a party of friends and acquaintances in one of the trendy studio apartments near Washington Square on the lower east side of Manhattan. Charlie brought some beer, one of the girls brought wine. Someone brought some hash and someone else brought some acid to get high on the music. One of the guys rolled a mixture of Cherry Blend pipe tobacco and hashish into a clumsy fat cigarette held together by spit and passed it around during the good part of Samuel Barber's *Adagio for Strings*. Yeah. Wow. Cool. Awesome. Did you hear that? Yeah. Wow. Cool.

This wasn't Charlie's first time. When the girl sitting next to him passed him the joint, he took a drag deep into his lungs so that they were filled almost to the bursting point and let it out slowly without coughing. Then he handed the joint to the guy sitting on the other side of him.

Charlie was beginning to feel pretty mellow when he saw the air in front of him waver. No, it was more like shimmer, and then a small dark point appeared in the middle of the shimmering. Another point appeared and then another point. At first Charlie thought they might have been flies or gnats or mosquitos or something like that, but they seemed to be locked into their positions, in the middle of the air, unmoving. It was the strangest thing he'd ever seen. One of the points started to grow into a small ball, like a balloon inflating. The poles were dark violet, and the surface went through a rainbow progression, with a bright yellow line around the equator, and then deepening back to dark violet at the opposite pole. Other points were doing the same thing at the same time seemingly in complete synch with each other. The balls formed a straight line in the air that quickly rotated 45 degrees back and forth, like a pendulum or maybe like watching just one leg walking. The round balls joined each other becoming an oblong object in the air. Then it became a thin line suddenly, blinked into a vertical shimmering, and then disappeared.

Charlie asked the girl sitting next to him whether she had seen that. *Seen what?* she asked. Charlie turned to the guy on the other side of him and asked whether he'd seen it. The guy looked blankly at Charlie, who tried to describe what he had seen, but it wasn't like anything he'd ever seen before. The guy said *like wow ... cool ... man. You been droppin' acid or somethin'?* Charlie said no, he didn't think so, but maybe the hash *had* been laced with something. *Yeah, wow, awesome, cool,* the girl sitting next to him said. She took his hand. They stood up unsteadily and walked to the bedroom.

***

Adam Yerushalmi sat in the reception area of Professor Freindlischer's office. Professor Freindlischer was a hypnotist who specialized in helping people quit smoking. He had a fairly good success rate, or so they said, and seemed well thought of in the Tel Aviv area. In Israel, in spite of the fact that socialized medicine was considered pretty high up the scale compared to other countries around the world, even America, everybody who could afford it only went to the professors and heads of medical departments, instead of going to younger doctors and inexperienced interns.

The professor called Adam into his consulting room. He looked over Adam's paperwork mainly making sure that all the waiver clauses were signed. Adam was skeptical of this whole hypnosis thing. He'd tried a number of different treatments but none of them ever made a dent in his nicotine habit. He doubted he was suggestible (or gullible) enough to be hypnotized. He was his own man.

The professor came around from behind his desk to sit down in a chair next to Adam. He told Adam to relax. While the professor was talking to him, Adam could see the professor indistinctly out of the corner of his eye, but he was mostly conscious of the professor's voice. The voice slowly faded into the background of Adam's consciousness which remained crystal clear. The last thing Adam remembered being conscious of was wondering when this hypnotic trance state was supposed to kick in.

A siren started to sound, building up like a pianist stubbing all the keys with his thumb nail from the bass notes of the left side of the keyboard all the way up to the highest notes of the right side. The receptionist turned up the radio full volume and opened the door to the professor's consulting room, which was something she had been explicitly instructed never to do under any circumstances. The siren continued its insistent blaring.

The professor hurriedly attempted to snap Adam out of his trance state. "I will count backwards, from three to one, and when I say *one* you will wake up ... Three, two, one. Wake up, man!" he implored but Adam had not responded. The professor slapped Adam on the back of his shoulder and shouted, "Wake up, damn you!" The receptionist stood nervously in the doorway and shouted at the professor, "Carl, for God's sake! We've got to get to the shelter!"

Adam seemed to snap out of his trance state, but he didn't seem to know what was going on around him. The professor shouted at him to listen to the siren, there were incoming missiles from Gaza, and they all had to go down to the bomb shelter as quickly as possible.

They rushed out of the office without bothering to lock the doors and ran down two flights of stairs to the bomb shelter in the basement of the building. Just as the professor pushed Adam into the reinforced concrete shelter, a surface-to-air missile defense missile intercepted the incoming rocket high above the office building exploding less than ten meters away from the rocket. Twisted shards and grapefruit sized pieces of metal picked up speed in their fall to earth causing minor damage to some rooftops and the outer walls of buildings in the vicinity.

Adam thought he heard a heavy silence a few meters away from him as though all the sound had been sucked out of the space. Then he heard a small high-pitched "tink" noise, followed by a deeply rolling discordant blat that seemed to widen until he felt it viscerally buzz-saw through his mid-section. Just as quickly the sound contracted, becoming more harmonic, soft, and plucky like the short strings of a harp. Again, he heard the "tink" noise and then silence.

Adam asked the professor and the receptionist whether they had also heard the strange noises he had heard. They both looked at Adam oddly. Adam tried to tell the professor what he had heard but he had no words in Hebrew *or* in English to describe the shapes of the sounds, let alone the sounds themselves. The professor thought Adam might have suffered some sort of post-traumatic stress from the indelicate way the professor had had to wake Adam out of his trance. He'd seen it before in the Army. He suggested to Adam that he visit a doctor. Professor Freindlischer thanked God Adam had signed all the waiver clauses. The Hamas missile attack did not qualify as an act of God, but at least nobody could claim the professor had been negligent.

Adam went to see his family doctor and tried to explain to him what he had heard that day, still fumbling for words.

Adam asked the doctor for a pen and piece of paper and proceeded to draw pictures of the sounds. The doctor typed in "synesthesia" in the symptoms box of Adam's Patient's Record and printed out a referral for an MRI.

Adam's MRI appointment was scheduled three months later for 3:00 in the morning. The technician was courteous and rather attractive, to tell the truth. He had to wait an hour for the resident doctor to review the results and type up her professional opinion: no indications of pathology in any of the layers of the patient's brain that were imaged. No findings. Adam was instructed to return to the referring doctor for an interpretation of the results of the MRI scan.

Adam understood the MRI results and he knew what he heard.

***

Ibrahim bin Amin heard the roar of rockets launched from the open lot between his building and the neighboring building. He dropped the newspaper he'd been reading on the carpet and yelled to his wife, Jamilah, to grab their little daughter, Dalal, to run down the stairs to the tunnel entry the Hamas had recently built under their building. Dalal insisted they take her teddy bear, Kasim, too. Ibrahim scooped up Kasim in his hand and they rushed out of their apartment. Jamilah held Dalal in one arm and the hem of her chador with her other hand so as not to trip going down the stairs.

When they reached the ground floor Ibrahim tried to lift the heavy iron door covering the entrance to the tunnel, but it didn't budge a millimeter. Ibrahim grabbed Jamilah's arm and ran with her and Dalal frantically to the next building hoping there might be an open entrance to a tunnel.

There was but it was guarded by a hooded Hamas freedom fighter pointing his Kalashnikov at them. They froze in the entrance to the building. The freedom fighter pulled off his face mask and told Ibrahim it's him, Abdul bin Ali, they were at madras together when they were kids. Abdul opened the heavy iron door and motioned Ibrahim and his wife and daughter over to the ladder going down into the tunnel.

Ibrahim hugged Abdul gratefully and helped Jamilah find her footing on the top rung of the ladder. When she reached the tunnel floor below Ibrahim handed down Dalal into Jamilah's extended arms.

High above Gaza, hidden in the clouds, an Israeli jet pilot released a missile and guided it through his crosshairs and the precise coordinates his onboard system had received from the Central Command's integrated defense system calculated from the trajectory of one of the incoming Gazan rockets. The men who had launched the rocket were long gone but the cumbersome rocket launcher was still there in the pilot's sights. A yellow-red light suddenly filled the pilot's grid display and then cleared to reveal a crater where the rocket launcher had stood and two hills of rubble where the buildings had been.

There was a deafening blast that Ibrahim had felt before he heard it. He heard Jamilah and Dalal screaming below and saw Abdul's bare feet under a section of an upper floor that had collapsed on them. Then he lost consciousness.

Jamilah and Dalal were able to escape through another part of the tunnel. When she came outside, she ran back to the building where Ibrahim was buried under the rubble. Jamilah and Dalal screamed and keened for Allah or someone to help them. Finally some men came to try to dig through the rubble of the collapsed building to find Ibrahim and Abdul.

After several hours, it was late afternoon already, Jamilah remembered the muezzin's call to Asr prayer, the men found Abdul and Ibrahim. Abdul was pronounced dead, a shahid.

Ibrahim was bleeding profusely from a nasty gash on the side of his head, but he was still breathing. They lifted him onto a door from the mound of rubble and carried him to a pickup truck they had flagged down, and rushed him, along with Jamilah and Dalal, to a UN field hospital nearby.

Two days later, when Ibrahim regained consciousness, Jamilah and Dalal were by his side praising Allah for his greatness and his mercy.

The day after Ibrahim came to, while one of the NGO nurses was entertaining Dalal, Ibrahim whispered to Jamilah that something strange had happed to him during the time he had been buried under the rubble. Jamilah leaned close to hear his words. "I felt something protect me," he said softly.

"Allah be praised," Jamilah answered.

"No," Ibrahim said, "not Allah. Something else. I don't know what, but I felt it. It was like a large hand holding up a section of the roof that had fallen on me."

"Ibrahim, my beloved, that must have been the hand of Allah," Jamilah smiled at her husband.

"No, I don't think so," he said, "but who knows? Anyway, there was something else. The doctors told me my heart had stopped."

Jamilah turned pale.

Ibrahim took her hand and pressed it to his heart. He said, "I felt a young hand reach into my chest, without cutting it open, and take hold of my heart, squeezing it and releasing it, squeezing it and releasing it, until it began to pump my blood on its own."

"Allah be praised. Inshallah," Jamilah whispered.

***

Tink Blat sat on a bench in the park near his home watching his brother Zic play grzbll. The ptchr threw a slow bll toward a coordinate a meter above the plt next to Zic's feet. Zic slammed the bll with his bt with such power that it stood still in midair, but the sky expanded outward by a factor of 10,000 and everyone could see the stars winking in the night sky although it was the middle of the day.

Tink was eleven years old. He was in sixth grade. His older brother Zic was fourteen. He was in high school already and studying to be a mathematician.

Tink took his tesseract out of his pocket and expanded it so he could see the spheroid screen floating inside it. He loved watching it because there were an infinite (I josh you not) number of channels. Tink was supposed to be doing his homework on one of the educational channels, but he preferred to watch the hyposphere channels instead. His mother and father limited him to watching his favorite channels just two hours a day and only after completing his homework assignments. Besides, they didn't like the amount of violence Tink was watching. What they didn't know wouldn't hurt him.
He was watching the flattened characters running down some

stairs before a bomb fell on them.

"Hey Tink," Zic said sneaking up on Tink from inside. "You're supposed to be doing your homework. I wonder what Mom and Dad would say if they knew what channel you're watching."

Tink changed to his homework channel. "Don't you dare tell on me," he threatened, "or I'll tell them about the window you broke playing grzbll last week."

Tink looked at his assignment for today. Let's see. The sum of the interior angles of any triangle on a plane surface is ... 180 degrees, he said out loud. The sum of the interior angles of a triangle on a spherical surface is ... 180 x (1 + 4f) ... anything between 180 and 540 degrees. The sum of the interior angles of any tetrahedron on a plane surface is ... between 180 and 720 degrees. The sum of the interior angles of any hypertetrahedron or pentatope is ... 180 to 3600 degrees.

Tink looked around for his brother Zic to see whether he was watching him. Zic had gone back to play grzbll.

Tink flipped back to the hyposphere channel he'd been watching. One of the characters he had been interested in was buried in a building that had collapsed. Tink's eyes began to fill with tears when he saw that the character's heart had stopped beating. Tink couldn't bear it and reached into the spheroid screen with his hand. His arm appeared to him to become elongated and small. His arm became longer and thinner until he touched the character's dead heart, wrapped his fingers around it, squeezed it, and relaxed ... squeezed it and relaxed.

A Riddle for Shabbat

Tommy was carrying his grandfather's pale blue silk pouch with the prayer shawl inside. His grandfather was carrying Tommy on his shoulders. Tommy's other job was to make sure that the breeze didn't blow the kippa off his grandfather's head. After a while the older man sat down on a wooden bench under the fragrant bougainvillea and carefully lifted his grandson off his shoulders onto the bench beside him.

"Did you know that Israel is known for having the most interesting anthills in the whole wide world?" the older man asked the young boy who was very very good in all manner of sports.

"Really Saba?" Tommy asked, half frowning and half smiling, not sure whether his grandfather was telling him the truth or another one of his tall stories.

"Have you ever heard anyone claim differently?" the older man asked Tommy.

"Well, no," Tommy said, thinking back over all the claims he'd ever heard from anyone at all.

"Then it's a fact," his grandfather said with a tiny glint in his eye that only Tommy could see. "I've got a riddle for you."

"You do?" Tommy smiled in anticipation. He liked his grandfather's riddles because he always told Tommy the answer at the end and then Tommy could tell it to his friends, stumping them, since he wouldn't tell them the answer unless they were his best friends.

"Yes," his grandfather said. "It goes like this ... What is so big that you can put the whole world inside it?"

"Give me a clue," Tommy demanded after thinking a long moment.

"Well," the older man thought about the riddle and what he could give away without giving it away. "Its walls are indestructible no matter how strong you are or how hard you try to destroy them."

Tommy thought he could destroy anything. He made a muscle with his thin arm and insisted that his grandfather admire it, which he did. Tommy requested, "Another clue."

His grandfather searched around for another clue that would be a clue but not a clue at the same time. He found one and said, "It is very beautiful, but only to those with eyes to see."

Tommy was stumped. Everyone he knew had eyes to see. Then he thought about the little blind boy at the restaurant that one time. His parents had told him not to stare. Tommy asked for, "Another clue!"

Now his grandfather had run out of clues that were not clues and was left with only clues that were really clues. He said to himself, "nu ... shoen," as though he were waving a white flag, and then to Tommy, "at the very center of it are two silver candlestick holders with two tall white candles in them."

Tommy thought he knew the answer from the final clue but the other clues didn't make sense to him. He looked down at the ground and said, "I give up."

His grandfather smiled at him and said nothing.

"Nu .. Saba!" Tommy insisted.

The older man said, "The Sabbath."

Postscript
The real Tommy is far away in another land and his real grandfather misses him very much.

The Chocolate Shop

"What? You don't like chocolate anymore?" He asked them.

"No, Saba," Tommy was pulling away. "I still like chocolate. It's just that I don't want to go here."

The older man looked inside at the tables and chairs, the shelves of light and dark chocolates, the cloudy displays of ice creams and sherbets, and the nice-looking young girl holding the menus standing in the open doorway smiling at them. It looked like nothing had ever happened here. It looked like a perfect place to take his two grandkids for a holiday weekend.

Daniel was busy double-thumbing something on his smartphone and didn't seem to notice where he was at the moment.

"Why, Tommy?" he asked.

"Because," Tommy said.

Daniel stopped double-thumbing and explained, "He doesn't want to go inside because this is where those terrorists came in and shot and killed those four people."

Tommy nodded his head somberly, agreeing with his brother for a change.

"Oh," the older man said, "I see."

They walked over to the low wall surrounding the open square where kids were skating and riding their bikes. They all sat down facing the square with their backs to the chocolate shop only ten meters away.

"If the world is such a good place, why are there such bad people?" Tommy asked his Saba, which means "grampa" in our language.

"I ask myself that all the time," he replied. "If the world is such a bad place, why are there such good people as you kids and your parents?"

"That's not what he asked, Saba!" Daniel interjected. He was the wiser of the two brothers. He was going to be bar mitzvahed next month. A long time ago, when we lived in tents in the desert, that was when a boy became a man. He still felt like a kid though. "He said 'if the world is such a good place ...'"

"I know what he said, Daniel," the older man smiled. "I just wanted to show you both that reversing what he asked was also an interesting question."

Tommy said, "What I meant was why do bad things happen? Why can't we be protected from them?"

"Your parents, your brother and sisters, your grandparents, and everyone else who loves you want more than anything in the world to protect you from bad things," Saba said, "more than they would want to protect themselves."

"But what happens if you are not with us?" Daniel asked.

"That's why we try to keep you close to us when we go somewhere."

"What if the bad people are stronger than you?"

"Love gives good people strength they didn't know they had."

"What if they shoot you?"

"There will be good people around you who will try to protect you."

"What if they run away with their kids or what if they've been shot too?"

Saba was quiet for a few moments. He didn't really believe in God, but he didn't want to weaken their confidence. Neither did he want to lie to them.

Daniel asked, "Why do bad people do bad things anyway? Don't they know they're not good?"

Saba was thankful to be rescued from the previous line of questioning. "I don't believe they think they're doing anything wrong. Nobody does anything wrong intentionally. Everyone believes what he's doing is the right thing to do."

"How can anyone think killing an innocent person is the right thing to do?"

"Maybe we killed an innocent person whom they loved very much, like we love you, and they wanted revenge for what we did."

"Why would we do that? We don't go around killing children, women, or old people. Sorry, Saba."

"Maybe we killed an innocent person by accident when we were trying to kill terrorists."

"But who started it?"

"Nobody remembers. Everyone believes his enemies started it."

"But who really started it?"

"I don't know. It depends on who's doing the counting."

"Don't they know we wouldn't kill innocent people on purpose?"

"They don't care what we say or think. They just care about what we do, like us. We don't care what they say or think either, just what they do."

"Why do they think revenge is the right thing to do?"

"They think that revenge is a kind of justice, when no other form of justice is available to them, just like many of us do, and everyone believes that justice is the right thing to do."

"I wanted revenge when one of my classmates said I was too short to play basketball at recess," Tommy admitted.

"What did you do?"

"Well, at first, I wanted to punch him in the stomach."

"So, what did you do?"

"I threw the ball into the basket. Everybody laughed at that, and he said I could be on his team if I wanted."

"If only people could think of other things to do to get even, besides killing, that would be good," Daniel raised his finger wisely.

"Anybody up for an ice cream," Saba asked, standing up and stretching his arms and back, "somewhere else?"

"Yes!" they both answered.

The older man offered each his hand and they walked away from the chocolate shop on the square. He said a silent prayer to no one in particular that today wouldn't be the day and this would not be the place.

Venus de Milo

"What can I do for you?"

"Well, Professor Palmer, I've been browsing the Internet and came across your work on false memories and external indicators differentiating false and true memories," Axel answered the man sitting behind the oversized mahogany desk.

"That was based on research and clinical experience with childhood traumas such as those of rape or incest victims," the professor explained.

Axel laughed, "That's not my case, not that know of, at least that's not why I came to you. Something's been gnawing at me for the last few years now. Something that I took for granted since I was a child, something I believed to be true like the solidity of the ground I walk on."

"Please go on," the professor was skeptical but interested. The man sitting in the high back chair across from him seemed somewhat older than himself, physically fit, and not given to believing every passing nonsense.

"It's something that is of consequence only to me but none-the-less has considerable impact on me," Axel continued.

"What has been the impact on you?" the professor asked, looking for some classic symptom to latch onto.

"The impact on me has been to call into question all of my childhood memories related to my relationship with my birth mother," Axel answered, taking the time to choose the precise words.

"Your birth mother?" the professor repeated, raising his eyebrow.

"Yes," Axel explained, "that *would* deserve some elaboration. My father and mother divorced each other when I was seven years old. Dad remarried when I was nine. After some initial difficulties in accepting my new mother, I came to refer to her as "Mom" or "my mother", and to the woman who gave birth to me as '*my birth mother*' or '*my biological mother*'."

"How did your birth mother feel about your referring to her as that?" the professor probed, thinking he might be getting closer to the core issue.

"Sorry," Axel offered, "a little more elaboration is necessary. After my parents divorced, my birth mother also remarried. He was an army psychiatrist at the time, a nice enough man, although I didn't have much to do with him. At first, they lived just across the court from us in the same apartment complex my father and I lived in. Then they moved down south, a good day's drive from us. They came to visit me a couple times a year, sometimes staying at a motel in town, sometimes bringing me back to their home. He never stood between my birth mother and me. I remember him always in the background. Some years later he was transferred to the Philippines. Of course, my birth mother went with him. They were there three years. During that time, they adopted a little girl. I remember getting a photograph of her in a letter. She must have been two years old or so. She was awfully cute. Three days before they were supposed to be rotated back to the States, my birth mother was doing some shopping in town when she was hit by a car and died. I was thirteen at the time. Her husband returned home with the infant and a coffin. She was buried in a cemetery in his hometown. I never had any further contact with him."

"That was quite a story," the professor exhaled. "How did your birth mother's death make you feel?"

"I was devastated," Axel said, "but I got over it."

"How did you get over it?" the professor asked.

"That's the crux of the matter," Axel also exhaled. "I never inquired into why my parents had divorced, at least not until a year or two before my father passed away. I have memories of my mother taking a switch to me when I was two years old. I remember her walking out of our house with a suitcase, getting into a cab, and driving away. I remember her coming to visit me after she had remarried, my running to wrap my arms around her waist, and her arms hanging limp at her sides. Later, after I'd studied Art History at college, I started associating her with Venus de Milo, because she had no arms to wrap around me. I assumed she never really loved me. Maybe she loved me in the beginning, but sometime afterward stopped. I assumed that might have had something to do with my father divorcing her and getting custody of me. My father always loved me, as much as I loved him. Of that, there was never any doubt in my mind."

"So, what caused you to call into question your childhood memories related to the relationship with your birth mother?" the professor probed further. It seemed obvious that this man was self-analytical to a fault. He might have made a decent psychologist, he thought, although the professor didn't have much faith in psychologists with their talking therapies.

"A couple years before my father passed away, I took him out for a drive," Axel answered. "We ended up driving past our old home, which Dad sold soon after the divorce. I was in my sixties at the time. Dad had recently turned eighty. I stopped the car in front of the house and asked Dad why he'd divorced my birth mother. He told me it was because she didn't love him anymore, at least not the way he expected to be loved. I asked him what he meant, and he told me she had said she loved him like a brother. Was that the only reason? I asked. Well sure, he answered, I didn't want to be loved like a brother. I wanted to be loved like a lover, like a husband. I couldn't wrap my brain around that. I told him married love is multi-faceted. There are many aspects to love when you are attracted to a person but, at the same time, care for her deeply like a husband but also like a father or like a brother. The existence of one aspect doesn't preclude another aspect. Anyway, that's why I divorced her, Dad told me, turning red. That's the silliest reason for divorce I've ever heard, I said, and we drove on."

"Why did that cause you to question your childhood memories?" the professor asked Axel.

"A few years later," Axel said slowly, "a woman came across my name on one of the social networks I belong to, quite by chance, she explained in a private message. She identified herself as the Philippine infant my mother and her husband had adopted. She confirmed the details I remembered about my mother's second husband and the events surrounding her death. She said she had been rummaging around the attic of her adopted father's house soon after he'd passed away. She had stumbled on a shoe box full of returned unopened letters addressed to me. She apologized for opening one of the letters but, after I told her it was ok with me, she read me the letter.

The letter told me how much my mother had loved me and how much she missed me. The woman, my half-sister I guess, told me her father had talked about the divorce. He told her that my father had tricked or forced her to accept the conditions of the divorce. That was difficult for me to swallow since Dad had always been a gentle fair man, except when his back was against the wall; however, I could believe my grandfather was capable of being forceful to get his way. Dad had dropped out of college to elope with my mother, who came from a simple background, not that I cared an iota about that. My half-sister asked me what I wanted her to do with the box of letters. I told her I'd love for her to send them to me. She said she would. That's the last I ever heard from her. I looked for her on the social network and sent her a follow-up message, but she never responded to me. It might be because of my political views, I don't know."

"So how do you think I could help you?" the professor asked.

Axel looked into Professor Palmer's eyes and said, "After hearing Dad's explanation about why he had divorced my mom and then receiving those messages from my half-sister, I don't know what to believe about my childhood up to the age of seven. Did my birth mother love me, or did she not love me? How can I know what happened to me? How can I interpret what happened? How can I assimilate what happened? Were my memories my memories or were they implanted? If they were implanted, then when and by whom? The ground on which I walked as a child has disappeared from under my feet."

After a moment the professor asked Axel, "What is it that you think I can do for you?"

"Obviously you are a psychiatrist, so you probably don't put much stock in talk therapy," Axel replied. "So, I was thinking that, if you had experience with and access to a transcranial stimulator, say, a transcranial magnetic stimulator or a transcranial direct current stimulator, you might be able to do an fMRI of my head while showing me a picture of my mother and mapping the cells or regions that lit up. Then you could stimulate just those areas while I reported which memories popped up."

"A nice idea," the professor said, "but the TMS and the TDCS coils are only positioned for regions of the brain dealing with depression and other moods. Besides, what you're asking for is a function not approved for those devices by the FDA. What you are requesting would require deep brain stimulation, which would require open brain surgery while you are conscious. Are you sure you'd want to do that?"

Axel thought about the professor's words a long time before answering, "If it turned out that my memories were true and my mother didn't love me, I could deal with that. If it turned out that my memories were false, that they were implanted, I could deal with that too. What I couldn't deal with is thinking my mother didn't love me when she did. It's like a major chunk of my memory is missing, like I have amnesia, not being able to trust any of my childhood memories. So, yes, I'd be willing to undergo open brain surgery for the chance of getting back my childhood memories before I die."

The professor tried to talk Axel out of what he considered to be a rather frivolous discretionary but dangerous medical procedure. "We wouldn't be able to differentiate between a true memory and a false memory; neither could we be able to tell apart a self-acquired memory from an implanted memory."

Axel told the professor, "I'd be satisfied if you found a memory in which her arms are wrapped around me."

The professor told Axel to go home and think it over, talk to his wife and children about it, and then give him a call if that's what he's decided. In any case, an elective surgery such as this would take up to a year to schedule, what with all the real life-and-death cases requiring surgery.

Axel thanked Professor Palmer for his time and patience and promised to call him one way or the other.

*

The surgery was scheduled for 2:00 New Year's morning. He reported to the hospital reception desk the day before the surgery, accompanied by his wife and children. He was assigned a private room and told to don the hospital pajamas. The nurses stuck him and probed him. He was taken to get an EEG, EKG, X-Ray, MRI, and fMRI.

"Do you still want to go through with this?" the professor asked Axel.

"Yep," Axel answered.

"Can't you talk any sense into him," the professor asked Axel's wife, glancing also at Axel's sons.

"No," Axel's wife answered, her energy depleted. "Just make sure you bring him back to us, alive and functioning."

"You know open brain surgery is never a slam dunk and Axel signed a waiver form protecting the hospital and us from any liability if the procedure has complications," the professor said

"Yes, I know," she responded. "He explained you wouldn't perform the surgery if he didn't sign the waiver. We wouldn't sue you or the hospital if he were to wake up a vegetable or didn't wake up at all."

Axel's sons gathered closer around their mother, putting their hands on her shoulder.

A male nurse shaved Axel's head. His wife gasped. Then she stood up and bent over him, kissing him on the cheek. "I love you," she said. "See you on the other side."

"Good luck, Dad," the sons said and, one after the other, kissed their father.

The male nurse wheeled Axel out of the room and down the hall to the elevators.

*

The timeline bifurcated again, as it does every moment; after all, we live in a quantum multiverse.

In one universe Axel's surgery was a success in every way. The professor had stimulated a memory cell in Axel's brain that triggered a memory of when his mother had hugged him warmly.

In another universe Axel's surgery was a success but all the memories were of a mean cold-hearted mother who had no arms for hugging Axel.

In yet another universe Axel's surgery was not quite successful. The young doctor assisting the professor had been handed an unsterilized scalpel. There was an infection and the inflammation spread through Axel's brain. He went into a coma and, three days later, died; however, the professor had managed to trigger a memory of Axel's mother hugging him. Then he lost consciousness.

Message in a Bottle

Hello,

I know this message is written in a language that is not native to you. Neither is it native to me. I don't speak your native language and you probably don't speak mine. I hope that the language which I've selected for this message is common enough for the both of us to understand each other and to express our ideas.

I know nothing about you except that you are the one who has picked up the bottle and managed to coax this message out of it. You know nothing about me except that I am the one who wrote this message and stuffed it in the bottle. You may be asking yourself why I did it. I suppose it's because I wanted you to pick up the bottle and read the message, and I didn't know of any other way to get it to you, the message, that is; I don't care about the bottle, once you've retrieved the message.

I try to imagine you. I won't tell you what all I imagine about you because you'd probably think it's silly and it's probably all wrong.

If you've managed to get this far, I'll tell you what I believe about you. There are quite a few things about you that are similar to me. You love your children. So do I. I'd give my life for mine as you'd give your life for yours. You honor your parents and grandparents, even if they're no longer living. So do I. You'd do anything for your family, make sure they have everything they need, work long and hard for them. So would I. You want the best life possible for them. So do I.

You have friends who would give you the shirts off their backs and you'd do the same for them. Some of those friends are like family to you. So do I. So are friends for me.

The truth is you don't know everything. Neither do I. Nobody does. There are lots of things you know but there are lots of things you don't know. It's the same with me. The things you don't know, you have to guess at, you have to trust someone or something, you have to believe that it's true. It's the same with me.

But let's face it. We have our differences too.

Your leaders tell you bad things about us, that we are your enemies. Our leaders say the same things about you. The truth is some of us really are bad. I suspect that some of you are really bad too. Our leaders say we can't trust you. Do your leaders say the same about us? It's not just talk. Some of you have killed or injured some of us and some of us have killed or injured some of you. I don't know who started it. Do you know? We tell different stories. We have different histories. They all go back so far that nobody really knows for sure what is fact and what is fiction. They also go forward into rosy futures that can't all be true because some of them are mutually exclusive. It's a zero-sum game.

Our differences are real, but so are our similarities. Why is it that our differences seem to blind us to our similarities? I'm not saying we should ignore our differences. I am saying we should be motivated by our similarities to keep on looking for a way through the valley of the shadow of death, relying on understanding and empathy of and for each other, rather than fear and hatred. Don't wait for our leaders to lead us to peace. They won't. They can't. It is far easier for them to lead us to war. Peace won't come unless there's trust and trust will only come one by one, two by two, three by three ...

*

I wrote this message, put it in a plastic bottle, drove to the border between us, and threw it over the wall. I have no idea whether anyone on the other side picked up the bottle, pulled out the message, and read it. I waited for several hours but nobody threw the bottle back over the wall to our side.

*

The previous paragraph was slightly inaccurate. I was walking next to the wall on the border between us when I saw an object tossed over from the other side. It landed close by, and I saw it was a bottle. At first, I thought it was a Molotov cocktail or something similar. It didn't have a rag stuffed in the neck of the bottle or anything like that, but I did see what looked like a note inside the bottle. My curiosity overcame my caution, and I walked over to the bottle and extracted and read this note. It didn't know quite what to make of it or what to do with it.

*

The previous two paragraphs are untrue. As a matter of fact, this whole note business is complete fiction. I wrote it in the firm belief that there's no reason why it shouldn't be true sometime, somewhere, that someone might write a note like this and someone else might read it, that they might feel each other's pain and prayers and loves, that those prayers and successes and victories might no longer be at each other's expense.

Not that it makes any difference to a God who created the Universe and all things in it, but I am an Israeli Jew and those on the other side of the wall are mostly Palestinian Muslims.

The only prayers that reach God's ear are prayers for peace among all His creations.

The Two O'Clock

Professor Bartholomew Hartfeld sat in a tall leather backed chair behind a dark mahogany desk. He looked irritably at the clock on the wall opposite his desk. His 2:00 pm was late.

He flicked the button on the intercom. "Has my two o'clock called to say he'd be late?" Professor Hartfeld asked.

"No, sir," Marta answered.

"Please let me know the moment he arrives," the professor requested, "but have him wait in the waiting room for the time he made me wait."

"Yes sir," his secretary said.

Bartholomew's eyes scanned his consultation office to make sure that nothing was out of place, that everything was in order. The clock showed 2:05. He checked his watch which confirmed that it was indeed 2:05, actually closer to 2:06. His irritation increased.

The professor spied something crawling up the richly upholstered blue chaise lounge chair beside his desk. He squinted one eye to see better what kind of creature it was. After identifying the culprit, the professor slipped off his right Oxford shoe and, standing up with right shoe in hand, he hobbled over to the lounge chair.

The cockroach reached the top cushion and moved toward the center.

Bartholomew raised the heavy shoe above his shoulder,

taking careful aim in preparation to strike the disgusting insect. He hoped that his 2:00 o'clock wouldn't walk through the door exactly at this moment and see him, one shoe on and the other raised to strike a cockroach on his expensive chaise lounge.

Suddenly the cockroach flipped itself over onto its back so that it was facing Bartholomew and hissed, "Stay your hand, kind sir, I implore you! I am your 2:00 o'clock client. I apologize for my tardiness, but it takes a while to crawl under the door and make my way across your carpet and up your chaise lounge. I announced myself to your secretary, but she did not seem to hear me."

The professor was dumbfounded. Somebody must be playing a trick on him! He looked around the room again, trying to find the camera or recording device. He walked around the office, methodically checking behind every chair and underneath each piece of furniture. He even opened each of the drawers in his desk. Nothing seemed suspicious or untoward.

Bartholomew stumped back over to the chaise lounge and scrutinized the cockroach. The professor smirked jocularly for whoever might be watching him, asking the cockroach, "How do I know that it is you that is talking to me, and not some impish trickster with a hidden microphone nearby?"

"Ask me a question whose answer is six or less and a positive integer, and I will respond by raising my legs as appropriate," the cockroach hissed.

The professor thought a moment and asked brightly, "how many fingers am I holding up?"

The cockroach extended outward three legs, keeping its

remaining three legs folded over its abdomen.

The professor lowered one finger and the cockroach lowered one of its extended legs. Bartholomew thought to himself, well, whatever was going on, he'd play along. "Do you mind if I record our session," he asked perfunctorily. "It's something I do with all my clients for later review and analysis. I don't want to miss anything."

"I have no issue with that," the cockroach hissed. "I know how disgusting we are to you, but could you be so kind as to help me turn back over onto my abdomen? It's quite difficult for me to flip myself back over. I'm not as spry as I used to be."

The professor felt a little less disgusted by the cockroach than he had before. He didn't know why. Maybe it was the recognition of another conscious being, no matter what the form was, that stirred the soup of empathy. He slipped a sheet of yellow paper from his notepad carefully underneath the cockroach and held the sheet at a 45-degree angle so that it slipped down the page gently but with enough momentum that it was able to turn itself over.

"Thank you, Professor," the cockroach hissed.

"Happy to oblige," the professor said. He pulled one of the narrower chairs over to the chaise lounge, sat down, and turned on the recorder. "For the record," he began. "It is 2:15 pm, Tuesday, July 22, 1958. I am in session with Gregory Samuels. What seems to be the problem, Mr. Samuels?"

"Please call me Greg," the cockroach hissed. "I've been thinking a lot about suicide."

The professor made a note of that and paused a moment

before saying, "The mind entertains all the thoughts that are possible for it to think, but that doesn't mean that we have to act on every thought we think or let a particular thought take over control of our mind."

"I know that I don't have to act on every thought I have," Greg answered, "but I'm not so sure that I have the intellectual or emotional resources to prevent this particular thought from eclipsing all my other thoughts."

"I would imagine you to be somewhat lonely, possibly cut off from the care and support of family and comrades," the professor ventured.

"Not really," Greg explained. "Could you close the curtains and dim the lights a bit? I have 350 siblings and thousands of close friends. We get together as often as we can. Most of us are quite gregarious and decision-making is easier and less stressful when we're all together. The sex is good enough, I suppose ..."

The professor wrote down some more notes, looked directly at Greg, and asked, "Could you expand a bit on your last sentence?"

"About the sex?" Greg glanced back at the professor.

"Yes, the sex," the professor said.

Greg exhaled in a long hissing breath that almost turned into a whistle before answering. "It's not so bad, really. When we're ready for it, we give off a potent pungent pheromone so that willing partners may find each other. Then we have our courtship rituals, the usual posturing and stridulation. The copulation is both intense and prolonged. We go back to our friends who expect to hear all the intimate details about our partner, the courtship, and the copulation. The problem is that it seems so mechanical, so predictable, so meaningless. I feel like a damned fool."

"So, you don't engage in sex?" the professor asked incredulously.

"I do engage," Greg admitted, "but I don't run to my friends for debriefing or enthuse about it. In a word, it's not my ultimate experience."

The professor smiled wanly. "I suppose you just haven't met the ultimate partner."

Greg answered, "It's more than that. We've been living like this for the last 320 million years: hatching out of our egg casings with 30 to 40 siblings, all of us gulping air in our initial shock of existence, crawling out on our own, feeding on whatever is to be had, morphing into adults, congregating, copulating, impregnating, dropping egg casings, and dying. Da capo al fine. We'll probably continue living like this for the next 320 million years. There has to be something more than that."

"Except for hatching out of eggs, it sounds like a good description of the human condition," the professor said after a while.

"I beg of you," Greg implored, "don't make light of my plaints. I'm pouring out my soul to you. You are my last hope. After you, the long night of non-existence."

"I swear to you, my words were wrung from the depths of empathy for your plight," the professor chose his words carefully. "Is there nothing to which you look forward, for which you hope, to which you aspire?"

Greg spoke as if from another world. His words hissed out of him, "There is no beauty, no poetry, no aspiration or hope, no break in the boring continuity of existence, no lovely fictions to distract us from our dull repetitious lives."

The professor countered, "How can that be? You seem to me a poetic soul."

Greg explained, "Yes, that is my curse. I am the exception that proves the rule. I could be the Shakespeare of my species, another T.S. Eliot or Ezra Pound, an Yves Bonnefoy, and it would matter not an iota. Poetry's coin is not legal tender in our society. I recite my poems to crowds of thousands, even millions, but they don't even listen. They look at me dumbly and continue with their copulation and feeding on dung, or whatever the collective mind has decided this moment. I feel loneliest when I'm in such a crowd. It's unbearable. If only I could have this poetry somehow removed from my brain."

The professor scribbled notes as fast as he could. He raised the pencil to his lips and tapped the eraser against his lower teeth. When he became aware of what he was doing, he stopped and thought about what he had just heard. He asked, "I suppose it would be too much to expect that your species has doctors who understand the functions and anatomy of your brains, wouldn't it?"

"Unfortunately, we do not," Greg replied. "We don't have so many different roles. There are no doctors. We don't live more than a year or so, although I've heard of some of our distant cousins living as much as four or five years. If we get sick, we die and that's that. End of story."

The professor said, "It's 1958. We don't have the capability to do what you wished yet. We don't even know where poetry is located in our own brains, let alone in a … forgive me … cockroach's brain. Who knows when we'll be able to map out our own brains or understand how they work? It will probably be hit or miss a long time until we finally get it right. A miss might render you speechless, unable to walk, or kill you."

Greg hissed a long whistle of wonderment. "Why make the effort to stay alive as long as possible when life is so fraught with suffering and pain? It took an eternity before I was born. My life will end before I achieve anything worthwhile. Then I will be dead or non-existent for the rest of eternity. We are barely a blip on the vast radar of eternity. Why bother? Why continue after the fallacy has been uncovered?"

Professor Bartholomew Hartfeld glanced up at the clock on the wall. It was 2:50 pm. "I'm afraid our time for today's session is up," he said, not insensitively.

Greg flinched as if waking up from a dream, "Huh, what? Oh … yes," he recovered his initial presence of mind. "I had forgotten about the fifty-minute hour."

The professor added, "It seems like we've barely scratched the surface. There is much ground to cover." Then he asked kindly, "Would you like for me to have Marta schedule an appointment for next week?"

Greg hissed ever so softly, "No, I don't think so."

"Next week's session will be … shall we say … 'gratis'?" the professor offered most generously.

The cockroach crawled slowly toward the edge of the chaise

lounge and then down one of the legs to the carpet. "What will you do?" the professor expressed genuine concern over the fate of his small client. "Please, don't do anything drastic until we've had a chance to examine all the alternatives!" he implored.

The cockroach slowly made his way over the carpet until it reached the door and then crawled under it.

Marta's voice over the intercom broke the ensuing silence as she announced, "Your 3:00 o'clock is here, Professor Hartfeld."

The Café

From where she sat at a small round table in the center of the otherwise empty café a wave of quiet rippled outwards languidly in the heavy heat of the midsummer afternoon.

I didn't want to disturb the spell by entering the radius of that quiet, sitting down at a table too near, and opening my notebook as is my wont in such places to write my own predilections.

The book she read was beyond my ken as her exquisite fingers hid the faint letters of the title. The tea in the glass beside her book was certainly tepid, as the air above her tea was not hot enough to make the light around it tremble and waver.

I ordered my own tea from the sometimes waiter and dipped my nib into my notebook.

After my tea was delivered steaming heatedly from the glass set down in front of me by the waiter he disappeared, as was his wont, leaving us alone in the café as though we were the lone survivors of a shipwreck cast ashore on a desert island. I was intensely aware of her existence, though she seemed intensely unaware of mine.

Every so often she would turn a page of her book, setting her mouth primly with her eyebrows slightly arched as though she might have been a bit near-sighted. I couldn't decide whether the thick black framed eyeglasses enhanced her beauty, or she was lovely in spite of the eyeglasses. I thought she might have been a schoolmarm or possibly she played the cello.

The hours passed slowly, darkening the sky outside the café imperceptibly. The waiter seemed still disappeared until I happened to spot him, sitting at a table on the sidewalk outside beside the boulevard smoking a cigarette.

By now it was getting too dark inside the café for her to read her book. I had stopped writing in my notebook some time before. My tea was also tepid by now. I looked about for a light switch in the darkness but couldn't find one. Probably both of us looked intently at the waiter sitting in the darkness outside, the embers of his stubbed cigarette glowing between his fingers. Even if he'd cared to do so, he probably couldn't have seen our faces willing him to come in and turn on the lights of the café.

I heard her chair scrape across the floor away from the table and saw the darkness of her slim form stand up against the darkness of the café. I heard coins drop on the table. I could see her dark form wending its way between the tables holding onto each wooden chair she passed until she reached the lighter darkness outside the café. The glowing embers of the waiter's cigarette seemed about to fall onto the sidewalk.

I felt for my notebook, knocking against the tea glass. I stood up carefully, reached into my pocket, and dropped some coins onto the table, one of which rolled on its edge over the side of the table, falling in a small clatter on the floor.

I walked toward the lighter darkness of the boulevard outside the café. The waiter had again disappeared, leaving only his stubbed and crushed cigarette on the sidewalk next to the foot of the table where he had sat. There was a rolling metallic noise of shutters and bars closing up the café for the night.

I looked up and down the boulevard among the milling crowds of men and women. There was no sign of her at all.

I crossed the boulevard to the narrow alley where my hotel was.

The Treasure Chest

Our "mamad" (see reinforced security room) doubles as a TV room and contains bookshelves and a work niche. On the second shelf above the desk is a small chest reminiscent of a pirate's treasure chest. It contains most of the coins I had in my pockets while traveling through various countries.

Our grandchildren always ran straight to the *mamad,* stood beside the desk, pointing up at the chest of coins, begging me to bring it down to the floor so they could look at the coins, which I gladly did for them.

The oldest would open the latch and raise the lid. The youngest and the oldest would pick out coins and ask me, what coin is this, *Saba*? "Saba" is Hebrew for "Grampa". I would take the coin from the proffered hand and carefully examine the coin before handing it back.

"This one is a fifty new-pence coin with a profile of Elizabeth II from Britain." I remembered arriving in Darmstadt, Germany, as a soldier in the US Army back in June 1970. I had just been assigned as a legal clerk for the 10th Artillery Group. My commander sent me to attend a course in Military Law. I had no legal background at all, but I was the first non-com with a college degree to arrive at Headquarters Battery. The course was held at the base in Oberammergau, near the Austrian border. Oberammergau is famous for enacting a Passion Play about the life of Jesus once every decade. The play was performed during the week I attended the course.

One evening I attended a performance. I hardly spoke a word of German at the time. Besides that, I'm Jewish.

While I was watching the drama, I met a young woman named Cathy. She had studied Shakespeare in public school, and I had taken a course on the plays of Shakespeare at the university. We hit it off and exchanged addresses. We wrote each other and she invited me to come to visit her in Tottenham. I had a little money saved and had a weekend free.

I flew to England. I hopped a bus from Heathrow to London and looked for a train to Tottenham. She lived in a nice brownstone apartment. Her parents let me sleep overnight on the couch. In the morning, they packed us a basket of home-made pear wine and sandwiches and Cathy and I took a bus to Stonehenge for the day.

I handed the coin back to the waiting hand.

"What is this paper, *Saba*?" the other one asked. I took the bill and looked closely. "This is a French twenty franc note with a portrait of Claude Debussy, a composer, on it. It's not worth anything anymore. They use Euros now," I said. I remember taking a train to Paris one weekend. I found a hotel in an alley off a side-street a few blocks from the Seine River.

It was my first time in France. The only French I knew were the phrases in my small phrase book. I could ask where the toilet was or do you have a hotel room for me, but I couldn't understand the answers. I found a nice-looking restaurant. The table had 3 tablecloths on it. I had yet to learn that the more tablecloths on the table the more expensive the tab would be.

The waiter handed me a menu. I pointed at the first item on the menu. It was *pâté de cerveau* or some such. When it arrived, I found out it was cooked brain. I didn't touch it. Fortunately, I had also ordered *vin rouge* (red wine).

I handed back the coin.

"What is this coin, *Saba*?" the oldest asked. "This one is a Dutch ten-cent Euro coin," I answered, handing it back, remembering one weekend I had traveled to Amsterdam by train. When we arrived, I was walking on the platform toward the station exits, when a young guy stopped me and asked whether I needed a place to stay. I hesitated. After a moment, I said yes. He seemed friendly enough. He said his girlfriend ran a hotel in the middle of town and he could take me there. I said ok.

I followed him outside to his Volkswagen. We arrived at a pleasant little hotel. He introduced me to his girlfriend. I checked in and got a key to my room. I had a splitting headache and just wanted to lie down to sleep it off.

Soon there was knocking, laughing, and shouting outside my door. I opened the door. Someone told me we were all going into town together, and I should come along. That's how friendly the Dutch were. When we arrived in the lobby, the girlfriend who owned the hotel looked at me and asked what's wrong. I told her about my headache, and she told me to sit down. She'd fix it. She put her fingers on my temples and, within moments, my headache dissipated - as though her fingers had sucked up all the pain. I was good to go. I thanked her and we joined the crowd leaving the hotel.

Our crowd merged with other crowds. It seemed as though all Amsterdam was walking up Canal Street, where the prostitutes displayed their wares in garish windows. We made our way somehow to just outside Cosmos, the biggest discotheque in Amsterdam. We couldn't get in because it was already at full capacity. The front door would open. The heavy bass would blast through the open door. One person would slip out sideways and another person would slip in the same way. The door would close behind him and there was only room on the street for everyone to sway in place to the thum-thum-thum beat of the bass coming through the closed windows.

"What's this coin, *Saba*?"

"It's one Swiss franc," I answered.

I remembered another weekend I had decided to visit Switzerland. I didn't have a US passport yet. All I had was my US Army green card so I couldn't cross the border legally.

Friday afternoon, after I got off duty, I hitchhiked down past Heidelberg and was let off at a truck stop in the Schwartzwald (Black Forest). My luck turned bad, and nobody stopped to pick me up from there. I looked around and found a truck parked next to the diner. Since the road was going south pretty much straight to the Swiss border without any turnoffs, I decided to climb into the back of a truck trailer and pulled some potato sacks over me. By the time the truck started moving, I was already sound asleep.

Sometime early next morning, I woke up. The truck had stopped and was waiting in line, probably to be weighed. I climbed out of the trailer and, under the cover of pre-dawn darkness, crossed the road and walked up a hill. After a few hundred yards, I passed a stone marker indicating that I had just entered Switzerland. I walked down the other side of the hill and into the outskirts of Basil.

I was able to hitch a ride all the way down to the picturesque old city of Bern with its castle walls and moat.

I hitched a ride back to Basil, had dinner and a beer, and slept near a stream in a field under the stars. In the morning, I went back the way I had entered, found the stone marker welcoming me back to Germany, and hitched rides back to my base in Darmstadt.

"Saba, what coin is this one?" the little one asked. It was one Deutsche mark. Memories engulfed me. A few weeks after I arrived in Darmstadt, I decided to teach myself German. I had dated an American girl who taught English in Darmstadt. She also volunteered to lead a discussion group of local Germans and Americans residing in Darmstadt. When she reached the end of her teaching contract and was about to return home, she asked me whether I would be willing to lead the German-American discussion group. Since the group only met one evening a month and my day job as a US Army legal clerk was not likely to interfere, I agreed.

For my first session, I brought a copy of Chaucer's Canterbury Tales, written in Old English, and read out loud the first line of the poem, "Whan that Aprill with his shoures soote". See Canterbury Tales General Prologue. The Germans understood it, but the Americans did not. We discussed how English had evolved from German. It was a lively discussion. I made many friends in that group, a minister and his wife from Gross Umstadt, and a few young soldiers (my age) in the German army (Bundeswehr). I made no secret of the fact that I am Jewish.

My German army friends took me with them to a popular discotheque ("Keller") in Darmstadt. American soldiers were not allowed in local discotheques because they had a bad reputation for getting ugly drunk and brawling. They gave me a membership card with my photo on it, so I wouldn't have any trouble getting in because of my US soldier's short-cut hair.

One evening I met a local girl at the *Keller*. Wilma and I danced all night. I offered to give her a ride home on the back of my Moped, a 50-cc motorbike. When we arrived at her apartment, she asked whether I could help her move her things from her old apartment to the one she had recently moved into. It was pretty late at night, but I agreed. By the time we had moved everything and arranged it all to Wilma's satisfaction, it was close to dawn. She invited me to stay over.

From that night on, I spent most of my free evenings with Wilma. I would ride my Moped back to our base around dawn, change into my fatigues, and stand for reveille each morning.

I wondered what ever happened to Wilma and Cathy.

"What about this coin, Saba?" This brought me out of my reveries. It was an Israeli one lira coin. Those went out of circulation a long time ago. My memories transported me back to 1968 when I was in my third year at Ohio State University.

It was a case of "love at second sight".

Talma's father was my stepmother's brother-in-law's cousin. My aunt and uncle lived nearby in Columbus. Talma lived in Israel. She was visiting my aunt and uncle. Mom and my aunt arranged a blind date for the two of us. Talma and I were the same age and we both attended university.

My parents invited Talma over to our Friday evening meal. Afterward, I took her to see "Guess Who's Coming to Dinner" with Spencer Tracy, Sidney Poitier, Katharine Hepburn, and Katharine Houghton. Our conversations were halting and clumsy, unlike the smooth and easy conversations she had with my parents. As Talma later told me, she liked my parents long before she liked me.

We didn't see or speak to each other again during her visit. There was no ill feeling between us. It was just a case in which Mom and my aunt tried to fit a round peg into a square hole.

Fast-forward to September 1971, during my last three months of active duty in Germany. I had two weeks of army furlough accumulated. I had heard that I could fly for free on any military flight as long as there was a seat available, and I showed my Army green card.

As a Diaspora Jew, since my *bar mitzvah,* I had always wanted to visit Israel. Germany was already halfway to Israel, and I didn't think I'd ever get a chance to visit the Promised Land. I had never been outside the United States except for a couple one-day excursions just over the border in Tijuana and Juarez.

When I mentioned my idea to visit Israel to my parents, Mom said to make sure I look up Talma and gave me her phone number. I said okay.

On my first day of vacation, I hitched a ride to Wiesbaden where there was a US Air Force base and looked for a plane going east. I showed my green card and boarded a plane to Naples, Italy. From there I found boarded a plane to Athens, Greece. From there I boarded a plane to Adana, Turkey. At the flight control desk, I asked whether there was a flight going to Israel. I was told, "Sorry, there was no such flight, but you can fly to Istanbul and buy an El Al ticket to Israel."

I had barely enough money to fly back to Rome and take a train back to Darmstadt. I resigned myself to the fact that, like Moses, I'd come so close to the Promised Land, but I would not be able to enter it.

I spread my sleeping bag on the floor near the desk and, after a while, fell asleep.

Toward morning, I heard two voices talking. One said he was going to visit his girlfriend in Tel Aviv. I opened my eyes and saw the two officers who were talking near me.

I got up and asked them whether they were flying to Israel and whether there was room for me on the flight. The pilot said, sure. I boarded a C-130 Hercules cargo jet. The seats faced backward. I strapped myself in. The flight was about forty-five minutes. We landed at Lod airport.

An Israeli army jeep took us around to the front of the airport. I found a telephone booth, bought a phone token, and called Talma's number. Her brother, Yechiel, answered. Talma was not home yet, but he gave me their address and explained to me which buses to take to get there. I did not speak any Hebrew except for a few prayers. Fortunately, Yechiel's English was good enough.

I boarded buses according to Yechiel's instructions. When I boarded the last bus and neared the intersection where I was supposed to get off, I stood up and squinted my eyes to see the street signs. A girl soldier asked me whether I needed help. I told her the name of the street where I had to get off. She got off with me and took me to the boulevard where Talma lived. I thanked her and asked her whether I could buy her an ice cream cone. She said no thanks and walked back to the bus stop to wait for the next bus.

There was a flower shop on the boulevard. I bought a bouquet, found Talma's apartment building, walked up the stairs, and knocked on the door.

When I saw Talma, it was love at second sight.

Toward evening, I asked whether there was a bench I could sleep on in the boulevard. Talma said there was no way I was going to sleep on a bench outside. I would sleep in her bed, and she would go to her grandmother's apartment a couple blocks away to sleep.

We were together every day for almost two weeks until it was time for me to return to Germany. She took me everywhere to see things in Israel that most tourists never see. We talked about everything and anything. Conversations flowed and intimacy grew.

On my last day in Israel, Talma drove me to the airport. She waited to see me off. I went to the information counter as I had been instructed to do by the C-130 pilot. The man at the counter said the flight had been delayed and I should return in two hours.

Talma and I decided to go for a swim and come back in two hours. When I returned to the information counter, the man said the plane had arrived earlier than expected. They had called my name over the loudspeakers. When I didn't respond, they took off without me. The next flight would be in another two weeks.

I had no choice but to purchase a ticket for a one-way flight on El Al to Rome. That was all I could afford. I boarded the plane.

When we landed in Rome, I purchased a train ticket to Munich. From Munich, I was able to scrabble together enough change to buy a train ticket to Darmstadt. When we got to Darmstadt, it was after 3 a.m.

I had six different currencies in my pocket, all of which added up to less than what I needed to take a cab to our base from the train station.

I walked to our base, changed into my fatigues, and presented myself for reveille just in time. Unfortunately, my hair had grown longer than military requirements allowed during the two weeks and my commander ordered me to write myself an Article Fifteen. I was the one who wrote Articles Fifteen for soldiers who had violated army rules according to the Uniform Code of Military Justice.

When I presented the Article on my commander's desk, he told me to forget it and make sure I got a haircut.

Talma and I wrote each other long letters almost every day. Declarations of love escalated.

In December, I was released from active duty and flown home. I went back to work for the same company I worked for before I was drafted. Talma and I continued to write each other. In one letter I asked her whether she would be willing to fly to Columbus and we would see how things went from there, no strings attached.

Talma arrived in March. I met her at the airport. She slept over at my aunt's home near us. We were together constantly. Later she moved to my parents' apartment where I was living.

One night I took her to my favorite park after hours when it was closed to the public. We walked along the trails to where they kept the raccoons. I was crazy with love for her.

I dropped down on one knee and asked her whether she would marry me. Incredibly, she said yes.

We married on May 14th, 1972. Our oldest son, Assaf, was born April 13, 1973. Ari was born February 27th, 1978.

A couple months later, on May 16th, we moved to Israel to a house Talma's parents had bought for us in Raanana. Ayal, our youngest son was born September 2nd, 1984.

As of this writing, our sons have blessed us with eight healthy wonderful grandchildren, ranging in age from four months to nineteen years.

Assaf has moved his family back to America.

I handed the coin back. Sometimes, they ask whether they can take a coin home with them. I say yes, of course, since I have the memories, but they always forget the coins when they go on to play with something else more interesting.

After they leave, everything is quiet. I pick up the coins, put them back in the chest, and put the chest back on the shelf for next time.

Dancing with Anna

I have learned to expect the unexpected from my wife, which is to say that I haven't a clue about what she is planning to do next. I, on the other hand, am totally predictable, which is interesting in that my wife and I come from completely different backgrounds. I'm talking about one hundred and eighty degrees different.

We are both seventy-four years young and we've stayed married for the last forty-nine years. Our marriage has spanned two continents, three sons, and eight grandchildren.

There have been good surprises and bad surprises, but even the bad surprises usually turned out good in the end.

A couple months before my seventy-fourth birthday, my wife asked me what gift I would like. Of course, I had no idea. There was nothing I needed or wanted. I usually don't have any ideas what gifts to buy anyone, including my wife. My taste in everything from flowers to dresses and jewelry leaves a lot to be desired. I can't tell the difference between a twenty-carat diamond and zircon or cut glass unless I drop it on a hard surface.

So, my wife asked me how I'd like to have a dance with Anna A.

I remember learning to dance with Miss Nagy when I was thirteen or fourteen. I learned to waltz, foxtrot, cha-cha, rock-and-roll, and even to twist. I took dates dancing during my high school years and danced in discotheques with girls I met when I was stationed in Germany in the Army. But my wife, who loves me dearly (I never could figure out why), said I couldn't dance. There were new dances, moves, whatever, that other people knew how to do, that I couldn't do or felt ridiculous doing. So, other than occasional slow dancing, I haven't danced for the last forty plus years.

We first saw Anna on a local television program called "Dancing with the Stars". She was beautiful, she was graceful, she was exotic, she was … Anna came to Israel from the former Soviet Union. She was born in 1982. She could have been our daughter.

Then there was this thing that happened. Maybe you heard of it? It was a global pandemic called Corona (not the beer). Along with the Corona, came masks, social distancing, contact tracing, isolation, and frequent and prolonged lockdowns in Israel and other enlightened countries.

Actors, singers, dancers, musicians, entertainers, newscasters, producers, directors, along with restaurant owners, pub owners, café owners, hall owners, and just about every other business owner you could think of - were out of business for the lost year of Corona. In order to survive, put food on the table, and pay the rent singers, musicians, and entertainers were willing to perform in your living rooms or backyards. There were dancers who advertised that they were willing to give private dancing lessons in peoples' homes.

So, when my wife asked me how I'd like to have a dance with Anna, I said yes, yes, YES! I think my wife was somewhat taken aback by my response. I thought to myself, *wrong answer. I should have said no, of course not … me dance? Not with anyone but my wife.* But my wife didn't flinch, and she didn't say, "Ha! I was only kidding." I think I dreamed about dancing with Anna that night.

A month or so passed. Unfortunately for me, Corona vaccines

were approved by regulators around the world, distributed to nursing stations, and jabbed into peoples' arms. Covid infection rates dropped like lemmings off a cliff and tentatively, but rather quickly, people came out into the sunshine and went back to work, performers performed for big audiences, and tickets were sold out.

With all that, my chance to dance with Anna evaporated like a mirage in a desert.

And my wife told me she was only kidding.

The Poetry Lesson

(a play inspired by Osip Mandelstam's "The Stalin Epigram")

The cell is pitch black except for two cones of stark light, one over a man wearing a sea-green single-breasted tunic, breeches, polished jackboots, and a peaked cap, sitting behind a metal desk, and the other over a naked man whose arms and legs are chained to a four-legged chair with one leg missing.

The first man asked, "Name?"

The second man answered, "Mikhail."

FM: Mikhail what?

SM: Mikhail Staklinsky.

FM: Profession?

SM: Poet.

FM: You really ought to take better care of yourself. You are far too thin to survive these kinds of things.

SM: Everyone tells me I am too thin but there's nothing I can do about it.

FM: Ahhh, yes ... Do you know why you are here?

SM: (*silence ... The second man's right earlobe has been cut off by a third man standing by him in the darkness and then the second man screams in short yelps, becoming a piercing shriek and then a howl quickly dying down. The first man records the decibels and the duration of the scream in the appropriate column of the protocol.*)

FM: Did you not hear my question? Maybe this will help you hear.

SM: I heard your question, but I wasn't sure how to answer.

FM: Before we go on, here are some ground rules. One … answer my questions; Two … you may scream if you wish but not while I'm talking. Simple, yes?

SM: Yes.

FM: Good, so why are you here?

SM: Is it because I wrote a poem uncomplimentary to our Comrade Leader?

The third man cuts off the second man's left earlobe. There is another scream, similar in decibels to the first scream but slightly shorter in duration.

FM: Ahhh, I almost forgot. Three … I ask the questions. You provide the answers. You may not answer a question with another question.

SM: I'm sorry … I didn't know … I am here because I wrote a poem uncomplimentary to our Comrade Leader.

FM: Actually, not. Just between the two of us, it wasn't a very good poem. I've seen far better. No, the reason you are here is to learn to write better poetry. It's simple, really. By the time you leave us, you'll be writing proper poetry.

First Lesson: choose the subject. Given the times we're in, it should be full of pathos, but not pathetic, a tragic figure fit for an epic poem.

You should try to come up with someone …

SM: (*silence … The third man observes the first man's cue and relishes snipping off the little finger of the second man's left hand. The scream is different in key and nuance. The first man is a connoisseur of such things, and the third man is a virtuoso.)*

The young boy lay in a pool of blood / In the middle of the cobblestone road …

FM: No, no … too common. Try to be original.

SM: The old man and his wife stood on the open windowsill / Holding hands as the door …

FM: No, no … an epic poem should inspire the reader.

SM: A naked man whose arms and legs / Were chained to an unsteady chair …

FM: That might work. It's always a good idea to write about something you know.

Second Lesson: choose a meter. I prefer the dactylic pentameter.

Why don't you try that in your poem?

SM: (*silence … The left ring-finger is unceremoniously cut off. The scream is broadcast to the other cells in the basement. The third man pockets the ring.*)

A naked man with his arms and legs chained in a dreadful place, / Fleeing his soul rides a stallion across open steppes freely

FM: Not bad … not bad at all.

Third Lesson: choose a rhyming scheme. My favorite is the Pushkin sonnet, you know, A-b-A-b-C-C-d-d-E-f-f-E-g-g

Why don't you give it a try?

SM: (*frantic silence as the first man searches the darkness for words to stave off his torture, that will hasten blessed death. His left middle finger twitches uncontrollably, knowing it will be next … He screams when it is cut off.*)

A naked man with his arms and legs chained in a dreadful place

Fleeing his soul rides a stallion across open steppes freely

Leaving his body to distant tormentors and death's embrace
His soul impervious to cutting no matter how deeply
Death unlocks chains and receives us like prodigal warriors
Honored by comrades, loved ones, and sprig-bearing lauriers
Torturers, what have they? Soulless they hopelessly wait for death
Unloved as locusts descending in a field of shibboleth
But maybe we do not differ so very much, you and I
Neither of us should ever have been born into this world of pain
Pain ergo sum, a faulty logic, so for whom is the gain?
Comrade will dream he's loved while I dream I am a butterfly,
The bullet will come as an old friend but unexpectedly
Promising to restore me to my former integrity.

After some time passed, the first man stood up, reached for his greatcoat, and joined the third man who had packed up his tools in a suitcase and waited by the door.

An indeterminate time later, two men entered the cell, picked up the chair with the second man still chained to it, and carried the man back to his cell, heaving the chair and man inside. The two men unchained the naked man and took the chair and chains with them, locking the cell behind them.

Death did not come to the naked man like an old friend that night.

It was destined for another cell.

Skinny Mick

Skinny Mick sat alone at his computer, logging into his multiplayer reality game.

He carefully chose a musclebound avatar, named Rip Scorn to bear his lonely soul on a perilous venture.

Fat Minnie sat alone at her laptop and logged into her multiplayer reality game too.

She carefully chose a beautiful avatar, named Liv Morningstar, to bear her soul on a romantic tryst.

Rip and Liv met in a bar. She was twirling a little pink umbrella from her little pink drink and Rip noticed the empty barstool, winking at him in the violet strobe light.

"Is this seat taken, sweetness?" He asked her.

"It is now, stud-looker," she answered.

The Deadbeats were playing so loud they had to text each other to talk.

Rip flexed a bicep and nonchalantly asked, "Would you like to get some fresh air?"

Liv surveyed the action behind her from the bar mirror and said, "Sure, why not?"

They left the bar and started walking in the direction of the river.

The streets were still wet from rain and reflected the neon storefront lights. The night skies were clearing, and it looked like they might be able to see some stars.

It seemed like they had been walking forever, but maybe it was because nobody spoke.

They saw a café up ahead that had a couple tables on the sidewalk. They sat down.

Rip turned up his jacket collar against the night chill and Liv pulled out a sweater from her handbag.

A waiter came and left and came back with two glasses of strong coffee.

Liv pulled a gold cigarette case out, picked out a thin brown cigarette, tapped it three times against the case, and asked Rip, "Do you mind?"

"Actually, yes," he replied.

She returned the cigarette to its case.

The waiter replaced the empty glasses with steaming glasses of thick black coffee.

They talked some, were silent some. Words didn't really matter, since they were all false, all part of their roles, things Rip or Liv would say.

The solid night sky began to crack open on the eastern horizon.

Liv reached for her handbag and said, "Well ..."

Rip reached out for her hand and said, "Wait ... What's your real name?" he asked.

"Why do you want to know?" she asked.

"I just want to know something that's true about you," he answered hesitantly.

"Just one thing?" she asked.

"Yes," he answered.

"My name is Minnie," she said.

"Mine is Mick," he said.

She said, "Nice to meet you, Mick" and disappeared.

Rip came back to the bar every evening, looking for Liv but someone else sat on her barstool and the barstool next to it was taken too.

He stepped outside into the rain-fresh night air and walked to the café.

He sat there until the crack of dawn, nursing his glass of coffee alone.

Every evening was the same.

Eventually he lost interest in the multiplayer reality game, closed the lid of his laptop, walked into the kitchen where his wife, Minnie, was watching something on the telly. He sat down and watched the show with her.

You know, the truth is, it's all samsara, but somehow, we make it bearable for each other.

The Dementia Diaries

1.
Just for the record, I didn't write this. My son did. He says he's recording everything I say to him on the phone, since he's so far away.
He says he's writing it like a poem, though I don't think my life is too poetic, and besides, the lines don't rhyme.
I didn't pick the title either. He says since he's recording everything, he gets to pick the title.
Maybe he's got dementia. I know I don't.

2.
What's this doing here?
I didn't say any of this stuff.
I don't need a diary. My memory's fine.

3.
Well, as long as you're asking, I'm not doing so well today.
Why? I'll tell you why.
They said they'd take me home today, and I'm still here waiting.
No, this isn't my home.
Who are they? They're the people who said they'd take me home.
No, it's not my home. My home is when I was a little girl with my parents and my sisters.
What do you mean they died long ago? I talk to Mama every day and they come to pick up Daddy every Shabbos, since they need him for a minyan.
My sisters don't call much. I guess they're busy doing things they want to do.
Why do you keep saying they are dead and buried in the cemetery with Dad?

I know that, but they're still alive since I talk to them every day. Would I lie to you?
Do I think you'd lie to me? No, I guess not. Maybe I'm losing my mind.

4.
I can only talk for a few minutes today.
Why? Because I've got to dress to go to work.
How *old* do I think I am? How old do *you* think I am?
I'm ninety-five?
So what? I have to pay my bills still.
What do you mean I don't have to work? What do you mean, "everything is paid for here?"
Very interesting, that's the first time anyone's told me that.
I'll just hop a bus and go downtown.
I read the syndicated news to the local rags and have lunch with the girls. It's the cat's meow.
Got to run.

5.
I don't know why you don't believe me that I work, and this place here is not my home. Just ask my Mama. She'll tell you.

6.
If what you say is true, and this is all I have, and all there is, and what I think is true is not, then what use is there in living?
Nobody comes to visit me or call. Nobody takes me anywhere or asks me if I'd like to go. My kids are far away. I don't see anyone, except these pictures on the wall.
No, I don't know any of the other residents.
The lady that kept a teddy-bear in her bag? The one with the trembly voice? No, I don't know anyone like that. Don't know anyone.
Maybe I'll hop a plane and come to you.

Dream Marriage

(*Inspired by Kurt Tong's "Dear Franklin"*)

This is a story about Thu Mai[1] and Joe Lee, a story ripped out of a Book of Life, a story told out of sequence, like unbound pages whisked away by a mischievous breeze.

Joe Lee didn't want to kill anyone or get killed either, but he painted watercolors like nobody's business. So, when the Marines drafted him, they made him a Gyrene artist. His job was to witness all the gore in all its glory and paint it for posterity. You may have seen that painting of his, of a naked little girl crying, walking away from a burning village hanging in the city museum.

Thu Mai came from a land where napalm-breathing dragons roamed the skies and bombs went off in the damnedest places, where the enemy was always closing in, like a noose slowly tightening around her family's necks.

Her parents stuffed all they could carry into a couple suitcases and paid dearly for a place in a frail boat, with a sail on the angry seas and a prayer that some freighter might see them, take pity, and rescue them, like some message in a bottle, cast upon the waves.

Joe somehow survived that war, if you call nightmares every night and shakes during the day surviving. He couldn't do much painting after that. He wasn't any good at work and not much fun on dates.

---

[1] *Thu Mai* means "Autumn Plum Flower" in Vietnamese

Thu Mai's parents thanked the local gods and their intervening ancestors when a freighter churned toward them, though it almost swallowed them in the suck of its undercurrent. They prayed everything would just keep still till they could grasp the proffered ladder that kept coming close and then jerking away in the bobbing and swaying of the waves.

The sailors gave them warm blankets, food and tea, a place to sleep, and let them off at a San Francisco dock.

Joe wasn't good for much of anything, but he started writing poetry at night and found a job during the day as a computer tech to pay his bills.

He met this girl at a park nearby, and as the thread of life unravelled slowly, the nightmares got less and less scary, and finally disappeared.

Joe married Beatrice, they had kids, and moved to New York. The kids grew up and had their own kids. Their lives were pretty comfortable with not too much to complain about.

Life was not easy for an immigrant family like Thu Mai's. Despite the taunts and threats, she got through school, went to college, and studied literature. Her mother tried to hold the family together, but she couldn't even keep herself intact.

One day Thu Mai came home, found her mother hanging from the bathroom doorknob, and her father died soon after.

Joe had read an ad in the local rag about a poetry reading at a downtown bar. He decided, what the hell, and went to listen.

Thu Mai moved to New York and found work translating poetry during the day, but at night she wrote her own poetry and read some of her poems at a local bar.

Joe sat in the darkness mesmerized by Thu Mai's voice whispered into the microphone, as she stood so lonely in that stark light cone. Married Joe, Father Joe, and Grampa Joe couldn't help but think about that voice, and fell in love with it as though he were young and single again.

Her voice softened into silence, and she descended into darkness, as the next poet was introduced.

After the last poet read his poem, an open mic was announced. Joe entered the cone of light, pulled a poem out of his pocket, and read it to the darkness.

Outside on the sidewalk Thu Mai was surrounded by fellow poets.

Joe walked around them and flagged down a cab to take him home.

One day, Thu Mai saw an ad in the paper about an exhibit of photos and paintings from her old country during the war. She usually avoided anything associated with those days and the old country. She didn't know why, but she decided to go.

She entered the revolving doors reluctantly and purchased a ticket. Thu Mai walked slowly from room to room, examining the photographs and reading the titles and descriptions of each one until she came to the painting of a naked little girl crying and walking away from a burning village, her grandparents' village.

Thu Mai felt naked again, though she was fully dressed, and she looked to see whether someone was watching her, but she was all alone.

Joe went back to that bar from time to time, when the poetry group was reading there. Often Thu Mai would read her poems too. Joe's spirit soared weightlessly those nights, but he loved Beatrice and the kids, and would never do anything to hurt them. Besides, he was old enough to be Thu Mai's father.

They exchanged emails and poetry. That's when Thu Mai saw his name and remembered the name on the painting at the museum, "Joe Lee". She told Joe she was the little girl, the one who was crying, in his painting. She visited him that night in a dream or a nightmare, Joe couldn't tell which.

Joe felt guilty for witnessing reality, while being detached from it and, once more, the dreams tormented him.

Thu Mai married a man who made her laugh, which was not a small thing, considering all she had gone through as a child, and she gave birth to a lovely haiku of a child.

Joe's dreams continued to oppress him, and he worried he might call out her name in his sleep. That day, he'd read a story about a ghost marriage in China and, in his dream that night, Joe married Thu Mai, just two ghosts drifting on a brain wave, under a moon, not hurting anybody.

The dreams continued almost every night, and Joe's wife, who lay beside him, felt happy he was sleeping more calmly.

During the days, Joe seemed more accessible and present when they were together, which was pretty much all the time.

When death finally came for Joe, it had a difficult time deciding whether to take him during the day or night, but in the end, it didn't really matter.

One-Eighth Cherokee Stories[2]

All along the Oconaluftee River Trail

All along the Oconaluftee River Trail, the trout were leaping but today, they leaped for the white man, not for us.

With bellies full and well-fed children, they take a seat and watch us enact our tragedy writ by white men, for white men and their spiritcatchers, not for us.

In the evening when the air turns cooler, we sit around, swapping old stories, and wonder how everything went wrong and why the mountains and the rivers hadn't warned us.

Sparrowhawk over the Creek

Sparrowhawk flew low over the creek as it wended its way between the rocks into the greying evening. He carried a plump grape between his teeth just to resist the crunch of it and the burst of its taste as long as he could. Soon the stars wheeled slowly overhead except for the polar star singing him home.

[2] The following stories are not authentic Cherokee stories, myths, or lore. They are fiction, the fruit of this author's imagination, written in what the author believes to be the spirit of Native American folklore. The "possible one-eighth" refers to the possibility that the author's great-grandmother might have been Cherokee.

Frogs on their lily pads looked up at the quick shadow of his wings and darted into the black waters while dragonflies ran across them, invisible to all but the sparrowhawk.

Goodnight, Sister Creek, Let Mother Moonlight cover you, he whispered.

The Dark Veil

Sparrowhawk had nowhere to go and nowhere he had to be. The breath of the mountain was cool and soothing, so he spread his wings suddenly to catch it in his warm places, and then, just as suddenly, returned them to his sides.

The mountains cast a dark veil over the sky and the stars pricked the veil, so that infinity could shine through. Sparrowhawk could taste the smell of leaves and stone, and fieldmouse, but belly was full of frog, and now was time to rest his head underneath his wing.

Timeless Mists

Long, long ago, in the timeless mists, when light was on one side and dark on the other, the future in front of him, and the past behind him, when explanations were simple, but it didn't matter if they were wrong, Sparrowhawk saw his *ga-li-tso-da-di*[3] down below.

---

[3] Cherokee word for "tent".

Smoke rose invitingly from the hole at the top of it and the painted hands on the outside said come home to his heart. He landed near the entrance and opened the flap, putting his head in the darkness, and whispered, *"Mother, Father, where are you?"*

Their faces swirled and stretched in the smoke and rose through the hole above toward the pin-pricked veil of night.

He went back through the flap and walked sadly, one foot after the other, unable to fly, to Sister Creek. He bent down to scoop some rushing water with his wrinkled hand into his dry mouth and saw his father looking back at him from underneath the water.

A Dog-eared Photograph

Sparrowhawk walked in silence up the golden path with his granddaughter toward the setting sun.

Ignoring the pain in his left wing, he cradled her in his arms and leaped skyward.

"Grandfather, what are you doing?" she asked, as they soared toward the westering mountains, caught in the center of a block universe like a dog-eared photograph of a bird in flight.

Sparrowhawk

Sparrowhawk stood on the mountain's edge, face set afire by the new dawn sun's singing. A wasp buzzed near the iris beside the path and an eagle flew heavenward unseeing until his muscles are too heavy and tired to pull the thick air under and behind him.

They say a man only needs three things to stand on his own in this world: a good heart, a long eye, and a swift foot.

Sparrowhawk Flew over the Wild Berry

Sparrowhawk flew over the wild berry on the path to old age with the taste of wakefulness in his mouth and turned his head to listen to the beauty and agony of the warm sun. He felt the wind rush through his wing feathers, cooling them.

A gecko nibbled a loquat fallen from its mother tree beside the path. He cocked an ear to the heavens, having heard sparrowhawk wings, and quickly ducked under a tree root before the talons closed on him.

The storm clouds, dark and heavy with rain, were still a long way off, but there are many miles between Sparrowhawk's parents and him.

Aliferous

Sparrowhawk didn't wonder what it was like to have wings. When he wanted to fly high in the sky, his arms became wings, and he rose and soared with the other hawks. When he wanted to hold something, his wings became arms to carry his loved ones or defend them against the wolves and foxes, and to draw pictures or write poems.

The pictures and poems didn't come like the sun or the moon, but like petrichor rising from the parched land during a light but long-awaited rainfall.

They came to him while flying and he'd hurry back to his nest to give them to his beloveds but all they wanted was succulent fish.

Where the Trees and Rivers Laugh

Sparrowhawk spoke to himself when he was alone, which was many moons since the young no longer heard and the elders no longer sang.

He said, fly away, Sparrowhawk, high and away, above the sun and the clouds, above the night to the land where the stories are true, and the people are too, and the mountains and trees and the rivers laugh, and smell like forever.

Where the elders went, I will follow.

As Stupid as Scarecrows

Sparrowhawk flew between the mountains toward the glinting sunrise and bluing sky, and down to the just awakened forest. As he walked over the gentle paths, he knew that he came from the same place that the trees and the mountains came from, and they weren't all that much different, except that they were silent and he talked too much, or so he thought.

The mountains and trees, and even the sun had feelings that he could feel and there was no need for words of explanation.

When they were hurt, they were angry or sad, and when they were hurt, people died.

Why didn't people understand this? Did people need the sun, the trees, and the mountains to explain this in words?

Sparrowhawk thought people must be as stupid as scarecrows and flew off.

Fear of Flying

When Sparrowhawk was just a little bird, barely out of his eggshell and feathers hardly dry, his mama and papa began telling him stories of flying, of soaring high, swooping low, and gliding on warm air currents.

Papa told him flying is impossible unless you believe you can do it. Then they didn't talk about it anymore.

Every day, papa would fly off and come back with worms or fish in his beak and put them in little bird's squealing beak.

One day, papa came back with fish and, flapping his wings, held it above little bird so that he had to flap his wings to rise up and snatch the fish from papa's beak.

The next day, papa came back and hovered higher, so that little bird had to flap more to get the fish, and on the third day, after a tasty meal, Papa asked little bird if he thought he could fly.

Little bird said no, but papa asked him, "Do you remember how you flapped your wings to get the fish from my beak?

Little bird said yes.

Papa said, "That's flying," and little bird said, "Oh."

Papa didn't push little bird out of the nest like all the other father-birds. He told little bird, "When you're ready, we'll fly together and I'll teach you how to catch the best fish, and we'll have a fine time together.

What Goes Out Comes Around

When Sparrowhawk was old enough to fly by himself and catch the best fish (he flew even higher than his papa), he always came home to his old nest to share the best morsels with his parents.

One day he spied a pretty bird during the Full Flower Moon. They made their own nest and under the Thunder Moon a new egg hatched.

One fine day when Sparrowhawk was looking for fish for his family in the river below, he saw papa bird and papa saw him. They didn't recognize each other, but he never forgot his papa teaching him to fly.

That was how he'd teach his baby-bird when that time would come.

The Levant Sparrowhawk

Sparrowhawk walked along the lower path of the Oconaluftee by the river, just before the break of dawn, when fish began to jump, and birds started singing their names.

Sparrowhawk whistled his secret name like the others, to scare his enemies and comfort his friends. The path began to rise through the cool smoke of the mountain ridge. The hunger yawned and stretched in his belly, and he wondered what would be for breakfast.

His wings pushed big gulps of air under him and lifted him high above the river. His eye spotted a trout jumping over a submerged rock and he fell like a silent arrow grabbing the fish with his talons before it finished its dive. Sparrowhawk rose again to the smoky sky, thrumping the air with his strong wings until he reached his perch overlooking the valley.

While he tore the flesh from the fish, he heard a distant *klee klee killy klee*! It seemed to come from behind the rising sun. Sparrowhawk dropped the trout and aimed for the sun rising over the eastern ridge. The sun began to rise above him and the *klee klee killy klee* dropped beneath the sun. He flew over ridge after ridge until the land under him flattened out and became a sandy shoreline.

The sun was well behind him when a vast sea spread underneath and his wings sang *klee klee killy klee* to keep flying over wave after wave, and night spilled over the vault of sky above, bringing the stars wheeling slowly around him with black rivers above him and below, and nowhere to rest his weary wings, except in Death, but *then klee klee killy klee* kept his wings thrumping, and everything disappeared except the thrumping and the *klee klee killy klee*.

A point of light and then a line appeared on the far horizon, and miraculously the sun rose into the sky, pushing away the night behind him, but as far as he could see, only waves rose beneath him.

The sun climbed over and behind him, and night came. Death licked his belly till there seemed nothing left to lick. Sun, waves, and night, over and over, for one hundred and thirty-seven days and nights. Every time the thrumping stopped, he heard the

Klee klee killy klee! But on this day, Sparrowhawk saw the pristine shore and the low hills behind it. Over the shoreline and the rocky hills, he flew and called *klee klee killy klee* to her. *Klee klee killy klee!*

And their hearts were quiet and pure.

Little Creek

Once there was a little creek that fed off Mother River when skies laughed so hard that they rained sweet tears. Because the creek was little and the fish were too, the gentle forest made a canopy to protect them from Father Sun's harsh heat when the skies stopped laughing.

Little Creek meandered through a gully among the hills of the people's village, which had been the people's home since time's memory began.

Little Brother and Little Sister lived with Mother and Father in a small hut in the village. Every morning after chores, they'd run and slide down the pebbly goat paths to Little Creek to laugh and duck and splash and swim with the little fish in the cool clear waters every morning.

Time also meandered in Little Creek and Little Brother and Little Sister went to sit with the elders after chores to learn their wisdom, but afterward they still ran down to Little Creek to laugh and duck and splash and swim with the little fish in the cool clear waters every day.

Little Brother and Little Sister grew up into Big Brother and Big Sister and each travelled far away, Big Brother to study Water Conservation and Big Sister to study Water Painting In big schools with many brothers and sisters.

They both returned once a week to Little Creek to laugh and duck and splash and swim with the little fish in the cool clear waters, but Big Brother saw the waters weren't as clear as he'd remembered and some dead fish floated aimlessly, making Big Brother and Big Sister not want to splash or laugh.

Time kept flowing, though Little Creek stood still and watched herself growing smaller and smaller and smaller.

Big Brother became full professor, giving advice to all the elders on Water Conservation

And Big Sister became a famous artist, painting scenes of creeks from memory.

One day, after many years had made them grey, Big Sister called Big Brother and said *Let's meet at Little Creek.*

They flew many hours in metal birds from East and West, meeting in a little airport. They rented a jeep and drove many hours to the hills above the gully where Little Creek meandered. They walked slowly, carefully down the pebbly goat paths to a dry cracked path strewn with twigs, pebbles, and little skeletons of fish where Little Creek once flowed.

No gentle forest canopy protected them from Father Sun's harsh heat, but soon it passed behind the western hills.

They buried Little Creek in their memories that night.

When Things Were Simpler

A thin wisp of fragrant smoke wafted up to the hole in the wigwam where the poles met.

The old man with the sunburnt face and sunken chest sucked air through the bowl of the pipe, making the tobacco turn bright red with quick intakes and passed the pipe across the fire to the young man sitting uncomfortably across from him.

"What can I do for you, Whitey?" the old man asked.

The young man took a puff and held his breath until he began to cough, and it was a long time before he could stop his coughing fit.

"I wish I could go back to times when things were simpler," the young man said.

The old man said, *"I'm a medicine man, not a charlatan."*

The young man went into a dream. Slowly the skin walls of the wigwam flew off the poles, and a panther and bear came closer to hear their conversation. Even the purple mountains inched closer.

"You can't go back to simpler times," the old man continued, *"because times were never simple. Many suns ago, when you were young, you had a child's mind. You couldn't hear other peoples' narratives, only the one your parents taught you, so you didn't know the conflict among them.*

"Your parents took responsibility for everything, so all you had to do was play with sticks and dolls. You never had to survive by wits and cunning.

"Life was never simple, though you thought it so, and it was the same when your parents were children, and when your parents' parents were children, back to when the earth gave birth to the moon.

"The more you learn, the more you see, the more you hear, the more you feel, the more you become aware of the complexities, so go back to your child's mind, if that is your predilection, or go forward and become a warrior."

The young man woke up from his dream and, looking around, the bear had become an old woman and the panther had melted into a little girl.

The purple mountains had moved back to a respectful distance and the old man was grinning with the pipe stem clamped between his teeth.

Wampum

"What is love?" they asked him.

"Love is what makes you feel alive," he answered, "the only thing that lets you know you're not dead yet."

"And what is life?" they asked.

"Life is that magic thing that happens when dead things get up and begin to dance," he said.

"And what is dance?" they asked.

"When we were young and full of life," he began, "we used to sing the memories of our parents and grandparents, and dance the old ones' stories.

"Nobody knows how to sing or dance anymore. The young ones just laugh at dancing and singing, and sit around with dead eyes."

The askers disappeared in the smoke of his pipe, which he tapped against the wall, till the burnt tobacco fell out.

All along the Mediterranean

The Horn of Thirst

There are only a few of us now, but once we were many, and the elders led us in their wisdom: the animals showed us the rivers and lakes and we shared our food with them. They ate us and we ate them.

The elders told us of the fruit that was everywhere and could fill our mouths with their juices.

They told us there was no hunger then, nor was there thirst.

"See everything and sing it to your children, that they will know and sing it to their kin," the elders said.

That was then.

Now the rivers and lakes are no more, the animals have disappeared, and the fruit is dry like a dead rhino's horn.

Last night we reached the lapping waters of land's end, too salty to drink, but this morning the sun rose over the red mountains in the distance.

One of us knows an elder song of green lands across a sea and sings it to us. We will be many again and we will meet ourselves in green lands, but we will not remember our songs and we will not recognize each other.

Someone else knows a song of binding sticks together to make a raft, and we sing it into the lapping water.

Daskalos and Aphrodite

One day in the ancient mists of forever, Daskalos asked the goddess Aphrodite what lessons could be learned from love, since Aphrodite was the goddess of love and Daskalos, the god of education. He said, I've seen humans and gods more intoxicated on love than on grapes crushed by Dionysus, I've seen others impervious to love, still others wounded by its arrows, and still, others who chose death to escape it.

For some, it is like a hearth that warms the home, for others it is like a conflagration that destroys all. Even for a single immortal or mortal, it can be all of these things, one after another in no particular order, like our dice games.

Should one abstain from love, stand strong against it, carry a shield for protection, or run from it as fast as possible? Should one approach carefully, warming hands and heart, or carry buckets of water to extinguish it? What should I tell those who would study love?

Aphrodite, who was studying her face intently in the mirror, while Daskalos blathered on, laughed and stood up from her throne, letting slip from her tunic the most beautiful breast that poor Daskalos had ever seen, and said, do not waste love's precious time by attempting to study her meandering ways.

No lesson can be learned, for even she knows not what she will do next, to whom, wherefrom, in what form or with what consequence. All you can do is play love's game of dice. After all, it's the gods' favorite game too and there is no life outside love's casino. Play or don't play, it's no matter to me.

Simmian of Locris

Simmian of Locris, not to be confused with Simmias of Thebes, was a little-known student of Socrates, who listened to the master's wisdom from a safe enough distance.

After the master transcended his earthly existence, by means of the hemlock offered him, Simmian left ancient Athens to see what he could see and to know what he could know.

Now Simmian knew many things, but there were still many more things he did not know. What loomed large on his philosophical horizon was the question, "what was he to do about all that he did not know?"

Simmian of Locris purchased a sea-worthy ship and an experienced crew and set sail for wherever the breezes would blow them.

The breezes began pleasantly enough, but sometimes they blew rather angrily.

After some difficult days and nights, Simmian's ship landed on the shores of a verdant green island with a rocky promontory.

Simmian set foot on the cool grasses and walked up a winding path, until he came to a wide plain with a thick forest to his right, and a stone castle to his left.

Coming out of the forest was a man wearing a crown and carrying a deer on his wide shoulders.

Simmian met the gentleman where their paths intersected.

"Good day, sir," said Simmian, "I come from the City of Locris."

"Good day to you," said the gentleman, "I can't say I've ever heard of Locris, but I'm King of this island, and you're welcome to sup with me."

"Thank you, kind sir," said Simmian, "But I just have one question and I'll be on my way."

The king said, "So ask your question, Locris."

Simmian asked, "How do you deal with what you don't know?"

The king answered, "Since what I don't know is fraught with unknown dangers, I built a strong castle with thick stone walls, a single thick door, and no windows."

"Isn't it rather dark inside," Simmian asked.

"I light torches and candles to see the walls and floor," the king answered.

Simmian thanked the king, went back to his ship, and set sail for wherever the winds would blow.

After more difficult days and nights, Simmian's ship landed on a sandy shore.

The shallow water was warm, as Simmian walked barefoot, carrying sandals in hand.

The sandy shore became wave upon wave of dunes mimicking the waves of the sea. He walked up and down the dunes with the sand escaping and refilling his footsteps.

In the distance was a small stand of fig trees, a stone well, and a man sitting against his camel in the shade of the fig tree.

Simmian approached the man at rest.

"Good day, sir," said Simmian, "I come from the City of Locris."

"Good day to you," said the man, "I can't say I've ever heard of Locris, but I'm Pasha of this land and you're welcome to sup with me."

"Thank you, kind sir," said Simmian, "But I just have one question and I'll be on my way."

The pasha said, "So ask your question, Locris."

Simmian asked, "How do you deal with what you don't know?"

The pasha answered, "Since what I don't know interests me more than what I know, I put up a flimsy tent wherever I happen to stay, poke holes in the sides to let the light in and let me see what goes on outside."

"On second thought, I've changed my mind," Simmian said, "I'd love to sup with you, kind sir, but I must go back to my ship and invite my crew."

And the pasha offered Simmian his camel, to speed his going and return.

After Simmian and his crew had stayed with the pasha three days and three nights, they thanked their kind host, returned to their ship, and set sail for wherever the winds would blow.

Eventually their ship returned to Athens, and Simmian sold his ship and paid his crew.

Simmian returned to Locris and opened up a shop to sell and repair sandals.

The Castle on Yon Promontory

Who could see the castle on yon promontory perched, hidden among the billowed clouds? Only knights of yore.

Nights of lore told by heroes of deeds heroic in battles of good against evil and the God-King, who sat on His invisible throne.

All alone was He, Him, no knight could see, but they felt His Sword's weight on their broad mailed shoulders.

God-failed soldiers marched forth against the hordes of the Evil Lord, arrows flying from both sides, spears piercing, and swords slashing.

Fears nursing widows' breasts, from windows keening wives and mothers.

What was, will be against all effort, seers cursing lemming quests.

Be Careful What You Wish

Να προσέχεις τι εύχεσαι …
Be careful what you wish …

There are those who would wish to live forever, those who wish they could remain the same age, or even go back to a prior age or return to a time they remember as being the best of times. *Be careful what you wish.*

There are those who would want to continue doing what they love doing now forever more, those who would want to stay with the one with whom they love being now forever and ever. *Be careful what you wish.*

There are those who would wish all their wishes to be granted without risk or effort, those who would wish all their wishes be granted as soon as they are thought of. *Be careful what you wish.*

To live forever would be to outlast our country, our world and our universe, even time itself.

To remain the same age is to have a body which betrays its experience.

To go back in time is to drag the universe backward with you.

To do the same thing over and over forever would be to make it predictable and boring to the point where it became torture, and to stay with someone forever would be the same.

To have wishes granted too easily diminishes their value, and to have wishes granted immediately, without considering consequences, can be deadly.

All things good have a beginning and end.

Only evil seems to stick around forever.

Tiresias

And they came to him, the poor and the rich, from every direction.

"Why have you come," he asked them

And they answered, "We hear you can see the future."

"Can't you see I am blind?" he asked and then said, *"But I can see a future."*

"Speak plainly," one demanded.

"There are many possible futures, but only one of them will happen," he said.

And they asked, "How can we know which will happen?"

He said, *"just as the present stands on top of the past, the future stands on top of the present."*

"So how do you know which future stands on top of the present?" one asked.

He answered, *"if we are to survive, it will be because one of us saved us from what would destroy us."*

"How can we know which one will save us?" they asked in unison.

"I don't know," he said sadly, *"I can only see a future. I am blind to the present, but I will tell you this: you kill your neighbors wantonly, as you kill the forests, the lakes, the animals, and the air.*

"How do you know that you haven't already killed the one who would have saved you?"

The people left quietly, one by one, each one looking for the one who would save them from themselves.

The Empty Streets of Haifa

Along the edges of the Ramon Crater, the old gazelles were not as nimble as they once were, but the shepherds were cognizant, shushing the storms on the horizon with their magic staves.

The irises on the cliffs over the Sea of Galilee swam in the soft breezes.

Wild boars crossed the Jordan River, wondering why the streets of Haifa were so empty while the overturned garbage cans seemed so inviting.

In the Distance, I Can See the Battlefields

I look out between the eucalyptus to the plains beyond and the brooding mountains shimmering in the East. In the distance, I can almost see the battles being fought: from the one side, we are overrun by history and it has taken us captive, every last man, woman, and child; we carry its terrible weight on our backs, its iron rings and chains drag us along, but from the other side, we are ambushed by the future, falling victims to its arrows and slings, doves fall from the skies, impaled among the olive trees and flags console the fallen with their flapping, the flapping foreseeing the coming storm.

Forethought

They called me Forethought, my parents, Iapetus and Clymene. I would still have been bound to that miserable rock with Zeus' fiendish eagle feasting on my emotions, if Heracles had not killed that hellish bird and released me from my torment.

At least I fared better than my Uncle Cronus, whom my crazy cousin, Zeus, murdered, his own father, for godless sake. What did I do to justify the wrath of Zeus? I stole a flame from his famous fire.

No fire was ever diminished by taking a flame, but I had no idea his flame came from Time's Fire, a fire colder than Death's final breath, a fire that does not consume, but is consumed like Life itself, withering Beauty and Loveliness the more it lives.

As I stared into the dancing flames catching the twigs, a young girl stepped out of the fire, beckoning me to come to her with her naked arms.

When I refused, she took a step toward me uncertainly, then another step, and then another. Each step she took, her eyes sunk deeper, her skin tightened, then loosened, sallow. Her bones protruded, and she bent over, aging before my disbelieving eyes, and collapsed in a shriveled heap at my feet.

Time, my human friends, is the revenge of the gods against mortal humanity.

The Death of Time

Forethought was too young to have a clue, though his method girded his ignorance.

He didn't understand that it's a god-eat-god world he was born into. I'm his father, I should know.

Uranus, we called him Father Sky, wedded and bedded his mother, Gaia, Mother Earth, who bore him six sons and six daughters.

I, they called me Iapetus, was one of the sons, and Cronus, the god of Time, was the youngest of them.

I guess all gods were jealous then, and Uranus was no exception. He locked up several of his sons in Tartarus down below. This made Gaia very angry, so she asked her free sons, who would castrate Father Sky with her sickle and free her sons in Tartarus?

Only Cronus agreed.

So, he used his mother's sickle to cut off his father's favorite organ and threw it into the roiling seas. Father Sky bled to death (it's probably just as well). Cronus freed his brothers leading them back aboveground and took his father's throne.

Cronus married his sister, Rhea. Limited gene pool was not a worry then, and the two of them begat Zeus and the other Olympians.

Now, Cronus grew jealous of his children and swallowed them as soon as they were born, except for Zeus. After Cronus swallowed eleven babes, Rhea figured out his *modus operandi*. She swaddled a boulder in a blanket, instead of baby Zeus, which Cronus gladly swallowed, boulder and swaddling.

When Zeus grew strong, he made his father regurgitate his brothers.

With the aid of his brothers and the Spear of Triam, Zeus put an end to Cronus and the Titans' rule.

Time stood still in all Olympus, except for one small campfire, in which the Fires of Time were allowed to burn. Zeus told Hephaestus, the crippled blacksmith god, to guard it from his son, Forethought, whom others called Prometheus, but Hephaestus was slow of thought and movement, And Zeus was preoccupied with affairs of his favorite organ.

Ah, those crackling flames would sputter and spit stolen moments, like furtive glances and forbidden thoughts, imagined lives in some alternate universe, Love's succubae and incubi, and accidental touches, as Hephaestus fed the flames with dry twigs and fanned them into dancing incantations.

Like all Greek tragedies, the end was known before the story began. His brother, Afterthought, consoled him, poor Prometheus, and his beloved race of humans.

Prometheus Unbound

Big as mountains they were, those Titans. When they walked the earth the ground shook and we all ran for cover, though nothing was safe.

They didn't seem to take notice of us. We must've been like ants to them, small ones at that, except for Prometheus. He always looked out for us, walked around or stepped over, so as not to step on us.

He even brought us fire. We already had fire from the lightning when it would strike the olive orchards sometimes, but we didn't want to hurt his feelings by saying so. It was true, though, we didn't know how to make it, so he showed us how, rubbing two sticks fast.

Of course, the fire from lightning is burning hot, but there's something strange about the fire that Prometheus brought down to us.

I didn't want to tell my wife about it, and I'm not sure whether I can trust you.

But a beautiful young maiden stepped out of it … and she was not wearing a stitch of

Tantalus in the Time of Corona

Sometimes I wonder how the ancient Greeks seemed to know all the fates to which we'd be doomed in some distant Hades, in some far-off time, like Tantalus for example, although I'd never serve my son for dinner, no matter who the guests were, but the punishment Zeus meted out to Tantalus for his, dare I say, culinary faux pas, was rather in extremis; that is to say, poor Tantalus was forced to stand in a pool of refreshing water, under a fulsome tree branch bearing luscious fruit, both of which receded when he'd try to reach for one or the other, the water or the fruit, and this was to continue until the end of his days, which, in Hades, never end.

So, what does his poor fate concern our days (and nights) of Corona?

We are condemned by epidemiology to social distance and masquerade, self-isolation, and stimulus deprivation, to see our loved ones via Zoom, to receive and send them hearts and smiley faces, but not to hold them in our hungry arms or kiss their luscious lips or cheeks, a home-bound Hades, tantalizing, as the ancient Greeks foresaw.

Psyche and Eros Revisited

As Freud taught us of the myths, we are condemned to re-enact them over and over, again and again, whether we know them or not.

We are Psyche and we are Eros, they are us.

Psyche will always light a candle to see Eros' face, while he dreams of Psyche and a drop of hot candle wax will always spill on his beloved skin, and Eros will always disappear, as in every tragedy where the fate is known, yet ineluctable, for what lover would not want her love to fill her eyes to the brim and thus, her heart and mind, and what loved one could stand the cruel tricks that the gods of Time and Death play on us all?

Were we to see behind the scenes, we'd know that Eros doesn't disappear – like us all, he ages and dies.

Love is always tragedy, and yet we keep on loving.

Agamemnon's Letter to Electra

Greetings, my lovely daughter, from the distant shores of Troy!

I can almost taste our victory - We have a plan, a subterfuge, but I cannot share it with you yet, lest their seeress, Cassandra, catch wind of it, but believe me, darling, it is cunning and audacious!

But enough of my dreary matters, tell me of yourself - I have heard you have grown in beauty since last you sat upon my lap, making braids of my unrepentant beard.

Of course, I love you more than life itself, more than my promised place in the eternal fields of Elysium, but you have your life and happiness ahead of you, a future much more worthy than a life with a worn old man who will worship you like the goddess you are for the rest of his short life.

Turn your lovely eyes away from me, toward one of your many suitors, to the one who pleases you most, who will protect you from all harm, even from the wrath of jealous gods.

Turn your eyes from me, my love, I cannot bear them any longer, they weigh so heavily upon my heart.

I hope to return home soon, to find you properly wedded with the promise of a little one in your belly.

Please convey my regards to your mother, Clytemnestra.

Love,

Father

Beshert[4]

Destiny is a funny thing, it wembles and wambles from nowhere you'd think to look, until it arrives at the exact place you'd never expect, and that's beshert.

If I'd never been born in America, I'd never have gone to live on the other side of the world, not me, maybe someone else, but not me.

And I ran free in the grassy fields under the gigantic skies of America the beautiful, the innocent, the ignorant of any and all things outside of its great self, where reality was measured in miles and feet, and only one language was spoken with a twang.

The *altneuland,* the old new promised land of Israel, destroyed by the Babylonians and the Romans, salt of the earth, not yet reincarnated, was my destiny, bashert, though I walked before it did.

If my father had not divorced my mother, my muse, who taught the woods to sing, the creeks to laugh, the skies to cry, and took another wife, Daughter of Hebrew school and contributor of coins to the pushka box, prayer of the Shema Yisroel and Next year in Jerusalem, I never would have built my home in the land of Israel, as it was beshert.

And if my now-can-I-call-you-mom and her sister had not introduced me to my beloved-to-be, who dreamed in her native Hebrew, Me, who had been dating blonde shiksas behind my mother's back until then, I never would have left my homeland for another, as it was beshert.

---

4 "Beshert" means *destiny* in Yiddish.

And if Uncle Sam's army had not sent me to Germany, I'd never have been able to fly for free to see my beloved in Israel, with love's crescendo bursting our hearts.

I'd never have carried back home those dare-devil dreams of Israel, as it was my destiny, beshert.

And if she had not come to America and loved me, me, the one whom no woman could love, and married me and bore me fine sons, and her father called her back home to the old new promised land, and where she would go, I would go, and where she would stay, I would stay, and her people would be my people, as it was with Ruth and Naomi, as it was my destiny, beshert.

Ashes

On a cloud high above us, shaped like a woolly lamb, ambling in a cyan sky, a soul stood before God, who told the soul it was time to be born on the world below, and the soul asked God, "Why me? Why now? I'm perfectly content to continue as I am.

And God answered, "There's an opening, April 19, 1943, that must be filled.

"Where this time?" the soul asked.

And God replied, "you may choose among Poland, Germany, Austria, Czechia, Slovakia, Netherlands, Italy, Greece, Hungary, Croatia, Serbia, Ukraine, Lithuania, Bulgaria, or Romania."

"Why not send me to Israel?" the soul suggested.

And God told the soul that Israel had not yet risen from the ashes.

"What am I to do?" asked the soul.

And God answered, "Bring the ashes."

Theme and Four Variations on a Middle Eastern Tale

Theme:
A scorpion met a tortoise on the bank of a wide river and begged for the tortoise to carry him on his back across the river to the other side.

"If I carry you," the tortoise said, "you will sting me, and we both will drown and die."

"Why would I sting you," the scorpion answered, "when my life depends on yours to cross?"

That made sense to the tortoise, who let the scorpion climb on his back and quickly entered the deep waters.

Halfway across the river, the scorpion stung the tortoise, who gasped, "Why?"

The scorpion said, "It's my nature."

Variation #1:
Scorpions are the chosen of Al-Scorpio, as written in the Holy Sands. They were here long before the tortoises, who are weak and hateful in His eyes.

A scorpion who kills a tortoise will ascend straight to heaven, and so the scorpion approached the tortoise on the bank of the wide river.

Variation #2:
Scorpions have been subjugated since before memory by the tortoises who stole their venom to sell for profit and use in

their ceremonies.

Scorpions, rise up against their evil by any means. Take back what is ours!

The scorpion approached the tortoise with stealth and cunning.

Variation #3:
Tortoises are the chosen of El-Tortoise, as written in the Holy Waters. They were here long before the scorpions, who are stupid and jealous of His glory.

El-Tortoise will protect us and keep us from the poisonous scorpions, and so the tortoise was surprised by the scorpion on the bank of the wide river.

Variation #4:
Tortoises are more evolved than scorpions, as proven by our science. We can swim across the waters and find new places to lay our eggs.

The scorpions may hate us in their envy, but they need us to cross the river.

And so, the tortoise was sympathetic to the scorpion on the bank of the river.

www.ingramcontent.com/pod-product-compliance
Lightning Source LLC
LaVergne TN
LVHW041102150826
845673LV00007B/1889

* 9 7 9 8 3 5 3 2 0 8 8 0 8 *